BY **Matt Brown**

# Mutant ZOMBIES Cursed My School Trip!

ILLUSTRATED BY PACO SORDO

USBORNE

# SUNDAY

# A VERY LONG
# LINE OF IANS

Ian Iansson was in a tight spot. In fact, as spots went, this one was tighter than a pair of the tiniest tightest tights stretched across the most colossally colossialest bottom.

He was sitting on a chair in the middle of a dingy, abandoned warehouse. His hands had been tied behind his back and no matter how hard he struggled, he couldn't seem to get free. He craned his head back to see what was behind him.

5

The chair was millimetres away from falling into a cavernous pit of deadly animals who all looked like they hadn't been fed for a while. A lion, three bears, a tiger and an enormous, bloodthirsty kangaroo all looked up, waiting for him to fall.

"There is no point trying to free yourself, Ian," said a voice from the shadows, dripping with danger. "The rope binding your hands is impossible to break. It is made from titanium and lasers and unbelievably strong glue like your grandad has in his kitchen drawer but won't ever let you use because it is SO strong and dangerous and would stick your fingers together, FOR EVER."

Ian wriggled his hands again. A bead of sweat trickled down his forehead.

A gigantic man appeared. He had a large mop of green hair and was wearing a white suit and tie.

"You! I might have known," said Ian.

"Yes, I must apologize for the inconvenience," said the man, pulling out a bright yellow feather from behind his back. "But I'm afraid that you have some information I need. And I happen to know that you have very ticklish feet."

Ian struggled again. It was true, he had the most ticklish feet in the world. The gigantic man moved closer to Ian. He waved the feather duster and laughed a horrible laugh. Ian closed his eyes.

"No, no, no, HHHHHEEEEEELLLLLL PPPPPP!"

"Ian? Ian?"

It was Ian's mum. She stood in the doorway to his bedroom and looked at Ian, who was sitting

on his desk chair with his hands behind his back.
There was a pile of cuddly toys behind him.

"What is it, my darling poppet?" she said.
"Whatever's wrong?"

Ian took his hands away from the back of the chair.

"Oh, er, sorry, Mum," said Ian. "I was, er, just playing."

Ian's mum looked around the room suspiciously. "I suppose he's in here, is he?" she said.

The gigantic man with the green hair stared at her. "I have a name, you know," the man said. "It's Remington Furious III and we were in the middle of a scene that you have just RUINED!"

9

Ian's mum completely ignored Remington Furious III.

"Because," she continued, "I thought that we'd had a talk about him and how you're a *teeny* bit old to have an imaginary friend."

Remington Furious III gasped.

"Ian, I simply cannot work in conditions like this," he said. "I'll see you later when *she* isn't here."

And with that he vanished in a puff of smoke.

Ian sighed.

"No, Mum, it's okay, he's not here," he said.

Ian's mum smiled.

"Good," she said. "I've told you before, you've got to stop using your imagination. It gets you worked up into a terrible lather."

Ian nodded slowly. He'd heard all this before but he couldn't help it – he had whole worlds that lived inside his head.

"Yes, Mum," he said.

"Like that time when you 'imagined' the house was being attacked by vampires. Remember?"

Ian nodded.

"I woke up to find you rubbing garlic all over yourself and trying to catapult my best silver jewellery across the room."

"I was trying to protect the house," protested Ian. "Everyone knows vampires hate garlic and silver."

11

Ian's mum stared at Ian.

"But it wasn't vampires was it, love?"

Ian's shoulders sagged.

"No, Mum," he said.

"It was a plastic carrier bag rustling in the tree outside your window, wasn't it?"

Ian looked at her.

"It was very dark," he said, quietly.

Ian's mum sighed and bustled over to his bed.

"Look, my little angel, there's so much going on in the real world that we don't need to waste our time making things up, do we?" she said, sitting down.

"No, Mum," said Ian.

"I used to have dreams, you know. I used to

12

imagine I could do things and go to exciting faraway places. But your granny used to say to me, 'Beverley, no good ever came of imagining things.' So, I stopped and married your father."

Ian's mum adjusted the sleeve of her grey jumper.

"Now," she said, a smile returning to her face. "I've been calling you for ages. Didn't you hear me?"

"Oh, er, sorry," said Ian. "I thought you might have wanted Dad."

Ian came from a long line of Ians. Ian's dad was called Ian, Ian's dad's dad was called Ian, Ian's dad's dad's dad was called Ian. In Ian's family, it was Ians as far as the eye could see.

Well, that's not quite true because Ian's dad's dad's dad's dad was called Derek, but no one liked him much anyway.

"Of course, I didn't want him, you silly sausage," said Ian's mum. "He was called into work an hour ago. Some sort of emergency involving an out-of-date cocktail sausage and a packet of continental meat slices."

Ian's dad worked for Widdle, the largest supermarket chain in the whole country.

"But he just called with the most wonderful news that I simply had to tell you about. Dad's got an interview on Tuesday. For a new job."

Ian felt a familiar knot tighten in his stomach.

"A new job?" he said. "Another one?"

"That's right, another new job." Ian's mum

14

nodded. "Isn't he clever?"

In the last six years, Ian's dad had worked in over thirteen different Widdle stores. They'd only recently moved to Dreary Inkling so that his dad could head up the deli counter at the out-of-town Mega Widdle.

"Your father said the job would be in the biggest Widdle in the whole country, which would mean we'd have to move again."

"But we've only been in this house for three weeks," said Ian, a familiar feeling of panic rippling through his body. "Dreary Inkling Primary is the third school I've been to this year. Nobody even knows my name properly yet."

But Ian's mum wasn't listening to him, she was gazing out of Ian's window.

"Won't it be the most exciting thing ever?" she said.

"Yes, Mum," said Ian, in a voice so quiet it didn't even really count as a voice at all.

# UNEXPECTED ITEM IN THE BAGGING AREA

Ian wandered into the spare room and looked at the cavernous suitcase that lay yawning open on the bed. A stack of freshly ironed T-shirts, shorts and other assorted clothes were piled in a perfect tower next to it. Suddenly, in a puff of smoke, Remington Furious III appeared. He was wearing a gold, sequinned spacesuit.

"So, what do you want to do now?" he said, brightly. "We could finish building that rocket and go to Mars?"

Ian shrugged his shoulders. "No thanks," he said, sitting down on the bed with a flump. "I've got to help pack for my school trip."

The perfect tower of clean and ironed clothes teetered and then toppled over.

"Do you think I'm too old to have an imaginary friend?" Ian asked.

Remington Furious III looked at Ian and smiled.

"I'm part of your imagination," he said. "I think what you think. The question is, do you think you're too old for an imaginary friend?"

Ian let out a big sigh.

"I don't know, maybe I am. But I never get the

18

chance to make any real friends because we move around so much."

Remington Furious III chuffled out a long, squeaky fart that sounded like air being let out of a party balloon.

"Do you remember when we first met," said Ian, "after the third time we'd moved house? There was a boy, Geoffrey Speen, who lived next door. I thought we could be friends because we both liked the same chewing gum flavours in the exact same order."

Remington Furious III smiled.

"Spearmint, peppermint, doublemint, triplemint, berrymint, mintymint," Remington said, blowing a huge spit bubble and letting it explode all over his face.

19

"But before I could get to know Geoff, Dad went and got a new job as Deputy Head of Biscuits in another store, and we moved away again."

"But that's when you started to imagine me," said Remington Furious III as he attempted to lick his own eyeball. "And now you always have someone to play with, right?"

Ian watched as Remington Furious III accidentally got his tongue stuck in his eye socket.

20

"I've only been going to this school for two weeks," he said, running his fingers along the zip of the suitcase. "I thought this trip might be a good chance for me to really get to know some people."

Remington Furious III stood up and pulled his tongue out of his eye with a loud POP.

"It'll be a brilliant chance," he said. "I could help you. We could workshop some friendship scenarios together."

But before even a whiff of any workshopping could take place, Ian's mum hurried into the room carrying an armful of pants and socks.

"Right then, my little pickled onion," she said. "Let's get packing."

Remington Furious III glared at Ian's mum.

"Well thanks very much for interrupting," he said. "We were actually just about to begin an exciting acting project. And now you've barged in like a stupid great big blundering pile of dog plops and spoiled it all. AGAIN!"

He walked over to Ian's mum, who had no idea he was there, picked his nose and smeared a trail of silvery snot right down the side of her face. Ian sniggered and Remington Furious III disappeared in a triumphant puff of smoke.

"Now then," said Ian's mum, who couldn't feel the snot trail because that was also part of Ian's imagination. "Shall we pack alphabetically or by body zone?"

"Mum, the school trip isn't until Tuesday. Do we really have to do this now?"

Ian's mum stopped sorting through socks and looked at him. She had a strange faraway look on her face. A bit like the sort of face Ian made when he went for a secret wee in the sea.

"It's the very first time you've ever spent a night away from home," she said. "How on earth are you going to cope without your mummy to look after you?"

She paused for a moment.

"It's not too late to change your mind, you know? You could back out if you wanted and stay here with me."

Ian sighed.

"Mum, I want to go. I'll be fine," he said. "I am nearly eleven years old. I can cope with being away from home for a couple of days."

Ian's mum was always acting like this, like he couldn't handle anything without her.

"Well, in that case, let's begin," she said, looking back at the clothes on the bed. "Pants."

She handed Ian seven pairs of pants.

"Seven pairs?" he said. "Are you sure? The trip only lasts two nights."

Ian's mum looked at him in horror.

"Two nights?" she said. "Good point, my little walnut whip. Better make it ten pairs. You never know when you'll need them."

Ian made a face and took the pants. He noticed his mum had packed a pair that had a cartoon alien, with the words TAKE ME TO YOUR TOILET written on the front. There was no way he'd be able to make friends if the person he was sharing a room with saw those, so he quickly hid them under the bed. As he put the rest of the pants in the suitcase he picked up a strange-looking bundle that was inside.

"What's this?"

"It's a special hand-hygiene parcel, just for you," said Ian's mum. "To make sure you're all clean and safe I've put in a mini, pump-action, hand-sanitizer gel dispenser. Wrapped around that is a packet of wipes to wipe the mini, pump-action, hand-sanitizer gel dispenser, and then wrapped around the wipes is a packet of extra wipes, to wipe the first packet of wipes."

Ian groaned inside. His mum always overreacted to everything and fussed around him all the time. Sometimes, Ian imagined that life would be so much easier if he was some sort of mutated human, who could remove his ears and pop them in his pocket so he didn't have to listen to her any more.

The sound of a car pulling up outside interrupted the chat about hand sanitizer.

"That'll be your father," said Ian's mum.

A minute later, the front door opened and Mr Iansson came rushing up the stairs and burst into the spare bedroom. His face was bright red, contrasting perfectly with his extremely green Widdle uniform.

"This is it, Bev," he said, unable to contain his excitement. "This is the flippin' big one."

Ian's mum clapped her hands together in anticipation.

"The job is to be the voice of the self-service checkout at the biggest store in the whole flippin' country," continued Ian's dad, smoothing down the few strands of straggly hair that he combed over his otherwise bald head. "They want someone to do the voice 'live'. I'd have to stand by the checkouts, with a sparkly suit and a microphone, and say

27

things. Get this..." He coughed and cleared his throat. "Unexpected item in the bagging area!"

Ian's mum clapped her hands again.

"Oh, Ian, that's wonderful," she said. "The job is as good as yours."

Ian's heart sank at the thought of his dad getting a new job and having to move again. He knew he had to do something that would show his parents how much he wanted to live in Dreary Inkling. Perhaps if he made some actual, real-life friends then his mum and dad would change their minds and decide to stay. But Dad's interview was in two days, which meant that the school trip could be his very last chance. It was a long shot but it was the only

28

shot he had. As Ian tossed the hand-hygiene parcel into the suitcase, he heard the distant rumble of thunder.

29

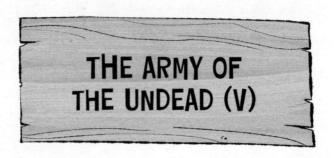

# THE ARMY OF
# THE UNDEAD (V)

A thin blanket of white mist, glowing in the light of the nearly-full moon, swirled and whiffled on the ground. A man with pale skin, the colour of bone, put down a lantern and leaned on a shovel. His dark, soulless eyes looked around the graveyard and a thin smile flickered across his lips. He heaved the shovel up to the lip of an unmarked stone tomb and began to prise off the lid. The sound of stone scraping against stone

30

echoed in the cold evening air before the lid finally clattered to the ground. Inside lay the body of a woman wearing a long black lace dress. The skin on her face was baggy and wrinkled. Her arms were crossed over her chest and her eyes were closed. The man reached into his long grey overcoat and pulled out a small silver flask. The eyes of the woman suddenly opened.

"'Tis time, m'lady," said the man, slowly unscrewing the cap of the flask before handing it to the woman.

She slowly sat up, her body creaking as she did, and took three large gulps. Colour immediately flushed into her cheeks and, around her neck, a jade-green amulet began to glow faintly.

"Delicious," she said, wiping her mouth with

the back of her hand, leaving a thin ribbon of slime flapping from her chin. "Dragon mucus?"

The man nodded.

"I ordered some in," he said.

The woman smiled and reached behind her head.

"Would you mind, Grimble?" she said, holding

up her long and tangled grey hair.

Grimble nodded and walked around behind her. He took an enormous clip out of his pocket, then grabbed a big, sagging flap of skin at the top of her neck and pulled hard. The wrinkles on the woman's face immediately disappeared. With a great effort Grimble opened the clip and snapped it shut to hold the skin in place.

"There," he grunted.

"How do I look?" said the woman.

"You look beautiful, as ever, m'lady," smarmed Mr Grimble. "Not a day over one hundred and three."

A laugh spluttered out of the woman's mouth.

"Oh, Grimble, you know very well I'm one hundred and twenty-six next birthday."

She rubbed her newly-smooth cheeks and smiled.

"So, tell me, Grimble, is everything as it should be?"

Grimble nodded.

"It is, m'lady."

"Good, good. So, when will our next victims be arriving?"

"In two days, m'lady."

The woman arched one eyebrow.

"And what sort of victims will they be?" she said, her eyes sparkling. "A coachload of old people, perhaps, come to look at a beautiful stately home on a day out? Or a group of business people, keen to take advantage of our team-building facilities?"

"No, no, our victims will be a group of schoolchildren," said Grimble. "They're coming for an overnight residential."

The woman smiled a hideous, wicked smile full of treachery and deceit, like a game-show host from hell.

"Splendid, Grimble," she said, looking up at the sky. "The moon is nearly full. In two days, we can try for a second time to create an army of the undead."

"Yes, m'lady," said Grimble.

The woman slowly rose out of the tomb and floated down onto the damp grass. The mist swirled around her ankles.

"And this time there will be no mistakes."

Grimble nervously rubbed his hands together.

36

"Er, no, m'lady."

"Not like last time, when you went and ruined my army of the undead, didn't you, Grimble?"

"Er, well, beetroot juice does look very similar to bat's blood and the kitchen was in such a mess," said Grimble, his bottom lip starting to wobble.

"Beetroot juice," said the woman, her voice rising in anger. "The spell asked for bat's blood and you used beetroot juice."

"I am very sorry, m'lady," said Grimble.

"And so instead of the spell creating a blood-thirsty army of the undead, capable of wreaking terror the world over, what did I end up with?"

"An army of vegetarian zombies," snivelled Grimble.

"That's right," said the woman. "A useless army of vegetarian zombies."

Grimble shuffled nervously from foot to foot.

"Urm, well, m'lady," he said. "They're not so bad. In fact, in many ways, vegetarian zombies are even better than normal zombies. They're ever so neat and tidy, they look great in sandals and they bake excellent flapjacks. It's just they're not overly fond of killing things."

Anger flashed across the woman's face.

"SILENCE, YOU FOOL!" she yelled. "ZOMBIES ARE NOT SUPPOSED TO BAKE FLAPJACKS! ZOMBIES ARE SUPPOSED TO EAT PEOPLE'S BRAINS!"

Grimble fell to his knees. "Oh, m'lady, I am so sorry. A thousand pardons. A million pardons."

"I am the great Gertrude Leviathan," snarled the woman, looking down at Grimble as he quivered at her feet. "And an army of the undead who don't like killing things is not what I need to take control of the earth. So, the next army of the undead had better be a proper army of the undead, otherwise

39

I'm going to melt you down for candles. I created you from a lump of my own earwax and I can just as easily turn you back again."

Gertrude Leviathan stared at Grimble with such a ferocious intensity that lightning began to crackle around her body and the green amulet glowed again. Slowly, Grimble's nose began to slip down his face, like he was a melting snowman, before plopping onto the floor.

"My nose," he moaned, holding his hands up to his face. "How will I smell?"

The woman looked at him for a moment.

"You will smell like you always do, Grimble," she said. "Like a sewage pipe, straight from the devil's own bottom."

Property of the Devil

# MONDAY

# A BIT TOO IAN-Y

After last night's rainstorm, the pavement that led up to Dreary Inkling Primary School was shiny and slick with puddles.

"Right then," said Ian. "Water is lava. If you step in a puddle, you're dead, or your foot burns off, or something really horrible happens."

"No problemo," said Remington Furious III, who was wearing a multicoloured school uniform and a pair of huge, gleaming silver boots. He bent

42

down and pushed a button on the heel of the boots and a tiny pair of golden wings folded out and began flapping furiously. A few seconds later Remington Furious III hovered ten centimetres off the ground.

"I won't be touching any puddles in these bad boys," he said, pointing to his boots.

Ian laughed and walked on, taking great care not to get any red-hot lava on his feet. It was then that he spotted one of the kids from his class, Haroun Nizami, crossing the road up ahead of him. Haroun was small, with a huge quiff of black hair and had an almost perfectly round face.

"Look!" said Ian. "Haroun has got a new rucksack and it's the exact same one as mine! Same make, same size, same colour. Look, it even

43

says 'I CARRY STUFF FOR A LEGEND' on it, just like mine."

"WOW!" said Remington Furious III.

Since joining the school a couple of weeks ago, Ian had thought that he would like to be friends with Haroun. He always looked happy, even when he'd forgotten to bring in his maths homework and Ms Husk had made him stay in at lunchtime to finish it.

"You know what this means?" said Ian.

Remington Furious III looked at him and nodded.

"RUCKSACK TWINS!" he bellowed. "That means you two could definitely be friends."

"Exactly," said Ian.

As Haroun crossed the road, he turned and

44

seemed to look straight at Ian and smile. Ian was just about to smile and wave back at him when he was overtaken by another of his classmates, Beano Lerwick. Ian sighed and his shoulders slumped. It was Beano who Haroun had been smiling at. He was another person that Ian wanted to be friends with. He was certain that he'd heard Beano say the words "Porkchop Vicarage" while he was queuing up for lunch last Friday. The Porkchop Vicarage was an area in Ian's favourite new videogame, TIME VACUUM, and he was desperate to talk about it, or maybe even play it, with someone. Someone who wasn't Remington Furious III. Someone real.

"Hold on, Hari," shouted Beano. "Wait for me."

He was munching on a doughnut and

45

accidentally knocked Ian as he went past, scattering hundreds and thousands onto Ian's shoulder.

"Oh, er, sorry, er, er..." he mumbled, trying to remember Ian's name.

"It's Ian," said Ian.

But Beano had already passed him and was sprinting towards Haroun, his springy mop of blonde hair bouncing as he ran.

Ian sighed.

"Ah well," he said, plodding on. "I suppose there's no point getting to know anyone, anyway. Even if we did become friends, Dad's going for this new job so we'll be moving again in a few weeks."

"You never know," said Remington Furious III. "He might not get the job."

"He always gets the job," said Ian.

Remington Furious III stopped hovering, landing back on the ground with a bump.

"I have just had a BRILLIANT idea," he said.

47

"Maybe the GREATEST IDEA IN THE HISTORY OF THE WORLD."

"What is it?" said Ian, skipping past a large puddle of lava on the pavement.

"Look," said Remington Furious III. "Maybe you need a change of image. I mean, look at you."

"What's wrong with me?" said Ian.

"Well, I don't know," said Remington Furious III. "You're just so Ian-like."

"But I am an Ian," said Ian.

"True, true," said Remington Furious III. "But maybe you're a bit too Ian-y. The problem is that no one realizes how AWESOME you are. If you had a change of image then you'd quickly become so popular that even if your dad gets the job then everyone in school would sign a petition for you

48

to stay. Or write to the local paper, or protest outside your house."

As Ian thought about what Remington Furious III had said, a large car sped through an enormous puddle by the side of the road, right next to Ian. A great wave of dirty puddle water sprayed him from head-to-toe. The driver of the car didn't even notice. Neither did Haroun and Beano who were now walking into school.

SPLASH!

49

Remington Furious III looked at Ian.

"Well, it's a start, I suppose," he said. "A seasonal blend of earthy tones. But I really think that your change of image needs to be a bit less wet."

Ian heard the bell ring for school and trudged through the school gates, dripping as he went.

50

# THE KID WHOSE NAME NO ONE COULD QUITE REMEMBER

Ian sat quietly in his seat by the window and listened to the register being taken.

"Lenny?"

"Here, Ms Husk," said Lenny Frisby.

Ms Husk ticked the register.

Ian looked around the classroom and imagined that everyone in his class was half-unicorn, half-human. They'd have a human top half and a unicorn bottom half but would have a horn

51

coming out of their forehead.

"Brianna?"

"Here, Ms Husk," said Brianna Grimditch.

Ms Husk ticked the register.

Ian wondered if being half-unicorn would make playing football easier or more difficult.

"Elton?"

"Here, Ms Husk," said Elton Gweek.

Ms Husk ticked the register.

Ian decided that by and large, being a unicorn/human hybrid would make playing football more difficult. Sure, you'd be faster because of the hooves but heading the ball would be almost impossible.

"Ian?"

Ian grinned, lost in his thoughts about unicorns puncturing footballs as they tried to head them.

"Ian?" repeated Ms Husk.

"Er, here, Ms Husk," said Ian, waking from his daydream.

Ms Husk took off her glasses and stared at him.

"I'm sorry?" she said.

Ian was aware that the whole class was looking at him.

"Er, I said 'here'," said Ian. "I'm Ian. Ian Iansson."

Ms Husk squinted at him, looked at the register and looked at Ian again.

"Oh yes," she said. "You started a couple of weeks ago, didn't you?"

But before Ian could say anything else, Ms Husk continued with the rest of the register. Once she had finished, she put down her pen and stood up.

"Now then, Year Six," she said. "Before we begin with our usual Monday morning maths, I have a couple of things I want to mention."

She looked around the room.

54

"First of all, I have just been informed by Mrs Tittering that two of your classmates are to be honoured by the Dreary Inkling mayor, the Right Worshipful Anita Goodparp. Eric Doomsday and Vinnie Mumbles, would you please stand up?"

Eric and Vinnie nervously stood up.

"You will remember," continued Ms Husk, "that only last week, Eric and Vinnie saved the entire world from being blown up by aliens."

A murmur flittered around the classroom. It had been a day of high excitement when two aliens had judged the school talent show before trying to vaporize the entire planet*.

---

* if you want to find out more, then the whole extraordinary tale is told in the thrillingly excellent book, *Aliens Invaded My Talent Show!* It really is the most tremendous value for money.

55

"Mayor Goodparp will be giving Eric and Vinnie the Freedom of Dreary Inkling, which is a very prestigious award that is only given to the cream of Dreary Inkling society," Ms Husk went on. "Although, Mayor Goodparp has asked me to remind you that the Freedom is restricted to the hours of 2.30 p.m. to 3.45 p.m. every other Tuesday and is non-refundable."

"Er, sounds really great," said Eric, looking at Vinnie and rolling his eyes.

"Yeah, great," said Vinnie, in a way that let everyone in the class know that she didn't think it was great at all.

"The good news is that the whole class has been invited to watch the ceremony at the town hall."

The class cheered at the news. Ms Husk held up her hands to quieten the commotion.

"Unfortunately, the ceremony is taking place on Wednesday afternoon, which means that we will all miss the big moment because we are going on our school residential trip to Leviathan Hall on Tuesday."

Ms Husk looked at Eric and Vinnie.

"I'm afraid it'll mean you two won't be coming on the trip," she said. "This award is just too prestigious for you to miss."

Eric and Vinnie shrugged awkwardly for a moment and then sat down.

"Now, the second thing I wanted to mention was that we need to sort out coach partners for our school residential," said Ms Husk. "I want

57

everyone to pair up with who they want to sit next to on the journey."

Ian suddenly felt cold sweat gather at the back of this neck. Had he been given some warning, he might have tried to catch the eye of Beano or Haroun and introduced himself properly. But everything happened so quickly that Ian simply didn't have a chance. The whole classroom erupted in a whirlwind of shouting and laughter as everyone ran around and sat with their preferred coach partners. After just thirty seconds of mayhem, everyone was sorted. Everyone except Ian. Nervously, he put his hand in the air.

"Yes, er, er, er..." said Ms Husk, looking straight at him.

"Ian," prompted Ian.

58

"Er, yes, Ian," said Ms Husk. "What do you want?"

"I haven't got a partner," he said.

Ms Husk counted up all the coach partners and saw that he was right. He was the one person in the whole of the class who didn't have anyone to sit next to. Ian knew this was bad. Very bad. The pairing up of coach partners was one of the most crucial aspects of any school trip. The journey could last several hours so it was important to sit next to someone fun.

"Don't worry, Liam," said Ms Husk. "You can sit with me."

"It's Ian," sighed Ian.

# CLEAN TOWELS, PILLOW MINTS AND BEETROOT SURPRISE

In the front drawing room of Leviathan Hall, Grimble stood and barked out orders.

"Sweep the staircase!"

"Polish the table!"

"Pick up that ear!"

And every time he barked, one of the numerous Leviathan Hall staff would jump up and rush off to complete the task. Well, actually that's not quite true. They didn't so much "jump up and rush" as

60

"moan quite a lot and shuffle around with their arms stretched out in front of them". You see, the Leviathan Hall staff were, in fact, the first army of the undead that Gertrude Leviathan had attempted to create. The vegetarian zombies that went wrong.

"How's the beetroot soup coming along, Keith?" said Grimble to one of the zombies.

"Soup good," said Keith. "Though, now it called Beetroot Surprise."

Grimble narrowed his eyes.

"What's the surprise?"

"While me make soup, some fingers fell off," said Keith, holding up his green-skinned hand to show that only his thumb and middle finger remained intact.

"What did you do with the fingers?" said Grimble.

"Nothing," said Keith. "Me left them in soup. That's the surprise for the kiddies."

As Keith moaned and shuffled back off towards the kitchen, the heavy wooden door of the drawing room creaked open and Gertrude Leviathan floated in. Grimble clapped his hands twice and the rest of the vegetarian zombies moaned out of the room to get on with their jobs. Gertrude Leviathan sat down in a large armchair next to a crackling fire. Grimble walked over to where his mistress was

sitting but stood on the opposite side of the chair, away from the fire. Even at this distance he could feel his waxen skin softening. Gertrude Leviathan snapped her head towards him.

"Is everything ready for the arrival of our 'guests'?" she rasped.

Grimble bowed.

"Everything is as it should be, m'lady."

Gertrude Leviathan's face creaked into a half-smile.

"Good, good. Well done, Grimble. Tell me, did you remember the clean towels?"

"Yes, m'lady," said Grimble. "Washed and ironed this very morn."

"And have you put the little mints on the pillows?"

Grimble nodded.

"Yes, m'lady, the tiny mints are in position."

"And the Great Curse? You have everything we need?"

Grimble nodded.

"Everything," he said.

The woman fixed him with her stare.

"Are you certain?" she said, a note of ice in her voice.

Grimble gulped and instinctively put his hands up to his nose. He didn't want to lose another one.

"Quite certain, m'lady," he said, nodding furiously. "There will be no mistakes this time."

The woman stretched her fingers and cracked her knuckles.

"Good, so our guests will be made comfortable?"

Grimble bowed again.

64

"Quite comfortable, m'lady."

The woman smiled.

"Well, comfortable to begin with anyway," she said, then threw back her head and howled a great roar of laughter. "AH HA HA HA HA HA HA HA HAAAAAAAAAAA!"

As she laughed, she rubbed the large green amulet that hung from her neck. She cast a sideways look at Grimble.

"Would you stoke the fire for me, Grimble?" she said. "My legs are very cold. I suppose that's what happens when you sleep in a tomb."

Grimble paused.

"Is there something wrong, Grimble?"

"Er, well, m'lady, it's just the heat of the fire, and me being made of, well, you know."

Gertrude Leviathan licked her lips.

"Don't you wish to do my bidding?" she said.
"Perhaps I should create another creature of the
night, one who is happy to do as I ask. Is that
what you would like?"

Grimble looked horrified and quickly bent
down towards the fire.

"No, of course not, m'lady."

He grabbed a poker and pushed the coals, making them spark and spit. After a few moments, he stood up. His face looked shiny and his skin had started to drip down his cheeks. Gertrude Leviathan stood up and slapped him on the back.

"Excellent, excellent, well done, Grimble," she said.

Grimble's head snapped forward with the force of the slap. He tried to put his hands up to his softened face but he was too late. Something small and round clattered on the stone floor like a marble. It rolled away into the darkness of the corner of the room.

"Er, permission to pick up my eyeball, m'lady, it seems to have popped out."

"Of course, Grimble, of course. But be quick, because if you don't find it then I'm certain the rats will."

68

# TUESDAY

# REAR GRAVE MAN

Ian walked through the Dreary Inkling school gates, struggling with his enormous suitcase.

His mum squeezed his hand tight.

"Will you be alright, poppet?" she said. "I'll be so worried about you, away from home for the very first time."

Ian looked at his mum. Remington Furious III was sitting on top of her shoulders in his purple, velvet travel-jumpsuit.

"You don't have to worry, Mum," said Ian. "I'll be fine. I'm looking forward to it."

Ian's mum patted him on his shoulder.

"My brave, brave soldier," she said.

Remington Furious III performed a series of perfect, rasping armpit-farts.

Ian and his mum walked over to where everyone had congregated, just outside the school's front door. Ian put down his suitcase with a sigh of relief. The three teachers who were coming on the trip, Ms Husk, the music teacher Mr Jagger, and the Year Six teaching assistant, Ms Fluther-Smack, were all nattering, chatting and laughing with some of the other parents. Most of the Year Six boys were running around, chanting, "COACH, COACH, COACH, COACH," over and over and over.

Ian looked and saw Haroun and Beano chatting by the railings. Beano was wearing a cool cap with a skull and crossbones on it. Haroun was wearing a white T-shirt that said I'M NOT LISTENING! on it, and an actual black leather jacket. Ian was going to go over but suddenly felt a bit ordinary in his boring jeans and grey T-shirt.

Ian's mum pulled out a brochure from her handbag. It had the words "Leviathan Hall" written on it and a photograph of an enormous stately home. The school had sent them to all the parents so they could see some of the facilities their children would be enjoying on the trip.

"This place sounds great," said Ian's mum. "It says here that Leviathan Hall is situated in a perfect rural setting, unspoiled and unchanged for centuries. The building itself oozes history and charm."

LEVIATHAN HALL

"Sounds like it's incredibly boring," muttered Ian under his breath.

"Apparently, there's an indoor swimming pool, a woodcrafting area, and a massage and relaxation room," Ian's mum went on. "It sounds lovely; I might come with you myself."

Ian's mum laughed at her own joke. Ian did not.

"YOU'RE NOT COMING, BOGBREATH!" shouted Remington Furious III. "IT'S NOT FOR MUMS."

"Just a note for the parents," said Ms Husk, looking around the schoolyard. "This is a history trip. We are going to Leviathan Hall to experience what life was like at a stately home hundreds of years ago. Because of this, no mobiles are permitted."

A groan went up from the playground.

"However, I will have my mobile with me and the number is on the information sheet. If there are any urgent messages or emergencies then feel free to send a text."

Ian's mum gave him a nudge.

"That's good," she said. "I can text you when I know about Dad's job. He has been called in for a special meeting about it today, which is a really great sign. It means that he's probably, almost certainly, bound to get it."

Ian felt the knot tighten in his stomach again just as a large, rusty-looking yellow coach swung into the school. There was a huge chorus of "COACH COACH COACH COACH" as it rattled through the playground and pulled to a stop right where Ms Husk was standing. It had once had DREARY INKLING TRAVEL COMPANY on the side, but now it was so old and so many letters had peeled off, it just said:

The door slowly hissed open and the driver walked down the steps. She was wearing dark glasses and had a walkie-talkie strapped to her belt, and looked more like a prison guard than a coach driver.

76

"Right," she said, pulling up her trousers and resting her hands on her belt. "Let's get a few fings straight before we start. No cans, no shoutin', no talkin' to the driver."

She whipped off her dark glasses, her eyes scanning everyone's face.

"And absolutely no singin', I HATE singin'," she added, before walking to the side of the coach and opening up a compartment. "Right, bags in here. NOW!"

A few minutes later, all the bags were safely stowed in the hold and the driver was back on board.

"Okay then," shouted Ms Husk, standing next to the open door. "When I call your names please make your way onto the bus and find a seat.

77

Hattie and Grace? Tom and Eddie?"

As the coach partnerships were announced, each pairing ran up the steps of the bus, laughing and screaming, and made for seats as close to the back as possible. Before long, only Ian was left. Ms Husk looked at him.

"Er, er, er," she stammered, flipping through some pages on her clipboard.

"It's Ian," said Ian.

"Right, right," said Ms Husk. "Ian, of course, of course, you're with me, aren't you? Hop on board then."

Mrs Iansson grabbed Ian by the shoulders and began kissing him repeatedly on the cheeks.

"Oh, Ian, Ian, Ian," she said, through streaming tears. "Be safe, my little pudding."

"Mum," Ian hissed. "You're embarrassing me."

"STOP EMBARRASSING HIM, WHIFFY," shouted Remington Furious III, doing a handstand on Ian's mum's shoulders.

Ian fought his way out of his mother's vice-like grip and walked up the steps of the coach, followed by Ms Husk. The door hissed shut behind them.

"We're over there, in those seats," said Ms Husk, pointing at two seats right next to the on-board toilet.

Ian walked over to them and sat down. Ms Husk sat down next to him and smiled.

"I've just remembered that I made some name badges for everyone," she said, slapping a sticky label on his chest with IAN written on it.

Ian looked at his name badge as the coach gears crunched and they slowly pulled out of the school playground and trundled off down the road. As the coach went over a speed bump, the toilet door banged open. Ian caught a whiff of something that smelled equal parts floor cleaner, runny cheese and rotten eggs. As he looked around, Ian noticed that he was the only one wearing a name badge.

# MR GRIMBLE

After what seemed to Ian like the longest journey
he had ever been on, ever, the Dreary Inkling
Travel Company coach finally turned off the main
road and spluttered up the enormous gravel drive
of Leviathan Hall. Ian looked out of the window
and saw a thick grey mist swirling around the
grounds, like it was trying to keep something
secret and hidden. As they approached the house,
Ian could see that ivy had covered most of the

front of the building and had even started growing through the small cracked windows.

"That's funny," he said, quietly. "It doesn't look at all like it does in the brochure."

The coach rattled up the drive and stopped in front of a flight of large steps that led up to the hall. Ian watched from behind his tiny coach curtain as a man emerged from the huge wooden front door and began walking down the steps. He had a wisp of hair, oversized, sticky-out ears and the palest skin Ian had ever seen. Ian couldn't stop staring at him. The man's eyes were dark and lifeless but danger lurked within them.

The coach stopped with a final shudder and, almost immediately, everyone jumped up from their seats to grab their stuff from the overhead shelf.

82

Everyone except Ian. He stayed in his seat and continued to watch the strange man from behind his curtain. He wore a suit the colour of midnight and shiny black shoes with long, pointed toes.

"Hmmm, nice threads," said Remington Furious III, who was now floating above Ian's head.

"EVERYONE, SIT DOWN," yelled Ms Husk.

The coach doors hissed open.

"HAROUN NIZAMI! STOP DOING THAT TO BEANO LERWICK," screamed Ms Husk.

Ian watched as the man began to walk towards the coach.

"BEANO LERWICK! STOP DOING THAT BACK TO HAROUN NIZAMI!"

Above the excited chatter and noise, Ian could hear each step as the man slowly climbed

84

on board the coach. He shivered as he saw the man appear next to the driver. It was like someone had just switched on the air-conditioning, full-blast. The man cleared his throat and everyone fell silent.

"Hello and welcome to Leviathan Hall," he said, in a voice that oozed like an oil slick. "We trust you will have a wonderful time with us for the next couple of days. I'm sure you'll find the experience –" he paused for a moment – "life changing."

Ms Husk was the first to speak.

"Er, thank you, Mister...?" she said.

"Oh, forgive me," said the strange man. "My name is Mr Grimble."

Mr Grimble bowed deeply. His wisp of hair

85

fluttered as he moved. Ian noticed that his skin had a waxy quality to it. It reminded him of his mum's favourite candle that she kept in the hall and only lit just before special guests came over. Then Ian jumped. He couldn't be certain but he thought he'd just seen a spider scuttle over the top of Mr Grimble's head and wriggle down the back of his coat. He looked around but no one else seemed to have noticed.

"Come, it is late and you have travelled far," said Mr Grimble. "I have arranged for your bags to be taken inside. Now, follow me and we can get you all settled into Leviathan Hall."

Ian shuddered as he watched Mr Grimble turn and walk down the steps of the coach.

Maybe it was the shock of seeing the spider,

86

or perhaps it was the creepiness of Mr Grimble's slippery voice, but there was definitely something that Ian found a little unsettling about Mr Grimble.

# A HISTORIC THING

Ian stood with all his classmates at the bottom of the stone steps that led up to Leviathan Hall. There was a quiet moaning sound coming from inside the stately home.

"What's that noise?" asked Luna Axminster.

Ian looked at Remington Furious III. "It sounds like the Northern Timeworms," he whispered.

Beano Lerwick turned around just in front of Ian.

"The Northern Timeworms?" he said, smiling. "From **TIME VACUUM**? You play it?"

Ian nodded. "All the time," he said. "Don't you think that noise sounds like when the Timeworms transport you through time?"

Beano listened to the moans, which were getting louder.

"Oh yeah," he said. "You're totally right. Nice one."

Ian smiled and was just about to try and talk more to Beano about **TIME VACUUM** when the source of the moaning appeared. Dozens of hooded figures slowly walked out of Leviathan Hall with their arms stretched out in front of them, their hands hidden by their enormous sleeves.

"Do not be alarmed by the staff here at Leviathan

89

Hall," said Mr Grimble. "They are dressed like servants would have been dressed when Leviathan Hall was first built over nine hundred years ago. It's a historic thing."

"A historic thing," repeated Ms Husk, looking at the other teachers. "Wow."

Ian watched as the Leviathan Hall staff staggered down the stone steps, took bags and

suitcases out of the coach's luggage compartment and carried them up to the house. And all the while they softly moaned.

"Are they alright?" said Ms Husk. "They're making quite a strange noise."

Mr Grimble looked nervously at Ms Husk and then at the Leviathan Hall staff.

"Er, yes they are all fine. The moaning is actually a form of medieval chanting," he said. "It's another historic thing."

Ms Husk looked impressed. She nudged Mr Jagger.

"Another historic thing," she said. "That is good, isn't it? Two historic things before we've even got into the Hall. We're certainly going to get an immersive experience here. I think—"

But no one got to hear what Ms Husk thought because she was interrupted by a suitcase clattering down the stairs, which nearly knocked Ian over. Everyone looked at the suitcase at Ian's feet, then turned and looked to the top of the stairs. One of the Leviathan Hall staff was standing there looking down.

92

"ME SORRY," he moaned, and began shuffling down the stairs to retrieve the case.

Mr Grimble smiled uneasily. "Don't worry, Keith," he said, through gritted teeth.

"Bag heavy," moaned Keith, picking up the suitcase. "Me tired."

As he began to heave the large suitcase back up the steps, Keith's enormous sleeve flapped open. Ian, and the rest of the class, saw that Keith's arm was a strange greeny-grey colour with patches of skin hanging off and flapping in the breeze. Everyone jumped back in shock at such a horrible sight.

"Er, please don't be alarmed," said Mr Grimble, smiling. "We have used make-up to recreate a skin disease that was popular among servants

93

when Leviathan Hall was first built."

Ian noticed that Mr Grimble's teeth were the same colour as his skin.

"Now, I am sorry but the owner of Leviathan Hall, Gertrude Leviathan, will not be able to join us today," he said, in a way that Ian thought was an attempt to change the subject.

Ian looked up at Leviathan Hall and, just for a second, he saw a shadow move at one of the upstairs windows. He thought he saw a faint green glow from behind the windowpane but the glass was so grimy that it was a bit tricky to tell.

"She is, er, feeling a little weak," continued Mr Grimble. "But she is very much looking forward to seeing you all soon. So, if you follow me, we can begin your exciting school trip."

Ian looked back up at the window but the shadow had disappeared. It left a troubled feeling flapping its wings inside Ian's tummy. He turned and walked up the steps. Ms Husk, Mr Jagger and Ms Fluther-Smack strode after him, while the rest of Ian's class followed behind.

"What was that up at the window?" whispered Ian, walking up the steps. "It was creepy, like someone was watching us."

95

"This whole place is creepy," said Remington Furious III. "It looks like the sort of house that should be owned by the devil or spooky ghosts or a bloodthirsty witch or something."

He looked at Ian. Ian shivered nervously.

"Er, although, I'm sure that it isn't," added Remington Furious III, disappearing in a puff of smoke.

At the top of the stone steps, Mr Grimble stood before the open front door.

"Welcome to Leviathan Hall," he said. "Please, come through."

And with that, he scurried inside and disappeared.

Ian stood at the top of the old stone steps and stared into the open doorway, which looked to him like it was a hungry mouth that wanted to swallow him whole. The air was cold so Ian pulled his coat tightly around him. He took a deep breath and followed his classmates inside. There was something very odd about Mr Grimble and Leviathan Hall – something Ian couldn't quite put his finger on.

# DAISY,
# THE LEVIATHAN
# FAMILY PET

If Ian thought it had been getting a bit chilly outside Leviathan Hall, it was nothing compared to how cold it was *inside* Leviathan Hall. He could see his breath in the air and hear the sound of chattering teeth as he nervously walked into a dark candle-lit hallway.

"Well, this place is an absolute DUMP!" said Remington Furious III, looking around the enormous hallway that led to a large wooden staircase. "You'll be telling me there's no electricity or Wi-Fi or anything like that next."

Mr Grimble coughed to get everyone's attention. "In case you were wondering," he said. "Leviathan Hall has no electricity or Wi-Fi or anything like that."

"WHAT???" shrieked Remington Furious III. "That is against my human rights." He paused. "If I was human."

"No Wi-Fi?" said Eddie Splott, as the sound of thirty gasps of astonishment echoed around the entrance hall.

"No electricity?" snorted Hattie Lavernock. "That's ridiculous."

Mr Grimble smiled at the bewilderment his statement had caused.

"We like to keep Leviathan Hall just as it has always been," he said. "So, it will seem a little darker than you're used to, but don't worry, your eyes will adjust."

"Well, that's no problem for us, is it, Year Six?" said Ms Husk, to a chorus of eleven-year-old groans. "It's a real treat to have an authentic historic experience like this."

Mr Grimble picked up a candelabra from a table. Ian noticed that he was wearing a large, black glove on the hand he used to pick up the candelabra. It looked a bit like the sort of gloves Ian's grandad, Ian, used when he was gardening.

"I thought we'd have a little tour of some of the facilities we offer at Leviathan Hall," said Mr Grimble, setting off down an extremely gloomy corridor. "Follow me, please."

Ian couldn't help thinking back to the brochure that his mum had been looking at earlier. Leviathan Hall didn't seem very charming. In fact, it just seemed really, really, really old and dusty and cold and dark. Mr Grimble stopped by a doorway.

"In here we have the indoor pool," he said, pushing the door open. "Please, go in and have a look."

Ian followed the crowd through the door and found himself in a room just as dark and cold and old as the rest of Leviathan Hall. Mr Grimble used his candelabra to light a torch that was hanging on the wall. Ian's classmates stood in complete silence at the sight of a large hole, in the middle of the floor, that was full of dark murky water.

"It's HIDEOUS and TOTALLY UNACCEPTABLE!" screamed Remington Furious III. "I'm off to see the manager."

And he disappeared in a puff of smoke.

"It's a very, er, basic, pool," said Ms Husk, nervously.

"It's from the thirteenth century," said Mr Grimble, "fed by a natural spring."

"Wow, a thirteenth century natural spring," said Ms Husk, who was obviously impressed with everything that was really old.

"W-w-what's that?" stammered Hattie Lavernock, pointing at the middle of the water-filled hole. "T-t-there's something in the water."

There was a collective gasp as everyone saw something roll over the surface of the water before disappearing back into the murky depths. Mr Grimble walked over to a wooden chest on the floor and pushed open the lid. From inside, he pulled out a dead rat, sniffed it and smiled.

"Daisy?" he called towards the water, waving the dead rat in the air.

Suddenly, a huge tentacle flopped out of the water. There were more gasps and screams and everyone moved a step back.

"Now, don't worry about Daisy," said Mr Grimble, tossing the rat into the air. The tentacle grabbed the airborne rodent and pulled it under the surface. "Gertrude Leviathan has spent years researching aquatic animals. Daisy is the result of one of her little experiments. She is quite harmless and is treated by Gertrude Leviathan as a family

104

pet. Daisy likes to use the indoor pool sometimes."

"I didn't realize that the Hall was such a seat of scientific learning," said Ms Husk.

Mr Grimble smiled, the spittle on his horrible greyish teeth sparkling in the candlelight.

"Oh yes, we love to experiment with things here at Leviathan Hall," he said, watching as the surface of the water started bubbling and churning.

Behind him, Ian could hear excited whispering. He turned around and saw Beano and Haroun smiling. When they saw Ian, they both shuffled closer.

"You know who Daisy looks like?" whispered Beano.

Ian nodded. He knew exactly who Daisy

looked like. He'd thought it the second he saw the tentacle.

"Joyce Crumble," he whispered.

Joyce Crumble was an end-of-level boss from **TIME VACUUM**. She was a Shoctopus, part shark, part octopus. In the game, Joyce Crumble travelled through timeholes. She roamed throughout time, using her enormous octopus tentacles to steal biscuits of great historic importance and scoff them in her massive sharky mouth. Beano began softly humming the **TIME VACUUM** music. Ian smiled and he and Haroun quietly joined in.

Suddenly, something flew out of the water and thwacked against the wall of the room. Ian, Beano and Haroun all turned and saw the skeleton of

the rat, picked absolutely clean, lying on the floor. Everything was quiet in the pool room before Drishya Samode broke the silence.

"That is SO awesome," she said. "Can I feed Daisy?"

A second later, the indoor pool room was echoing with the shouts of people wanting to throw dead rats into the water. Mr Grimble smiled and held up his hands.

"I'm afraid Daisy has had her food for today," he said. "Perhaps some of you could feed Daisy tomorrow. Now, who wants to eat?"

A great cheer erupted from the Dreary Inkling school party and Mr Grimble ushered them all out of the indoor pool room.

*This place is very weird*, Ian thought to himself

108

as he followed everyone back into the gloomy corridor.

Mr Grimble marched ahead.

"Now, the Leviathan dining room is over eight hundred years old," he said. "But don't worry, your food tonight was freshly made this morning."

Everyone laughed at Mr Grimble's joke and followed him happily. As they neared the entrance hall, they passed a door that Ian didn't remember seeing before. The door had a strange brass handle in the shape of a dragon's head. Ian stopped for a closer look and stared at the dragon's teeth.

"You must never, ever go through that door!"

Ian jumped and saw Mr Grimble was staring at him, a look of fury burning behind his eyes.

"No one must. NEVER EVER! EVER! EVER! EVER GO THROUGH THAT DOOR!"

There was an awkward silence for a moment.

"It's, er, just a toilet," Mr Grimble continued. "But it's out of action. It's, er, being, er, historically restored. SO STAY OUT!"

He stared at Ian for a bit longer, his wisp of hair gently fluttering in the cold breeze, then his mouth curled into a smile.

"Okay," said Mr Grimble. "Let's eat."

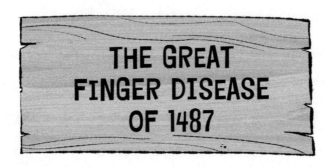

# THE GREAT
# FINGER DISEASE
# OF 1487

Ian took his seat at the enormous wooden table in the Leviathan Dining Room. He was sitting next to Ms Husk, who in turn was sitting next to Mr Jagger, Ms Fluther-Smack and Mr Grimble. Enormous bowls of food on large silver trays were brought to the table by the hooded waiters. Through the flickering candlelight, Ian watched as Mr Grimble spoke to one of the staff. Whatever was being said, Mr Grimble looked very angry, especially when the staff member shook their hooded head.

"Your attention, please," said Mr Grimble, tapping his glass with a spoon. "We hope that you enjoy your soup. It is based on a recipe that has been made in the kitchens at Leviathan Hall for the last three hundred years, so you'll be eating what people have eaten at Leviathan Hall since the reign of King George the First."

Ian noticed Ms Husk nodding with appreciation at this historic culinary news.

"Now, there is, er, a special surprise as you eat," continued Mr Grimble. "I have asked our kitchen staff to hide one or two, er, plastic fingers in the food tonight."

"Fingers?" muttered Ian. "That's weird."

"The fingers, er, are in the soup," continued Mr Grimble, "to reflect the, erm, Great Finger Disease of 1487."

"The Great Finger Disease?" said Ms Fluther-Smack. "I studied history at university. I don't recall reading about that."

Mr Grimble flashed a smile.

"It was, er, a very sudden and, er, localized plague," he said. "It ravaged Leviathan Hall one

113

Thursday afternoon, causing people's fingers to start falling off. We thought the fingers in the soup would be educational and fun."

The teachers all purred with delight at the thought of such detailed historical titbits.

Mr Grimble's eyes flickered around the room.

"And whoever finds the fingers," he said, "will win the opportunity to feed Daisy tomorrow morning."

Excited whispers fluttered around the hall as Ian's classmates discussed how cool it would be to feed Daisy. Mr Grimble sat down next to the teachers. Ian listened in to their conversation. He watched as Ms Husk picked up a glass, took a swig and laughed at something Mr Jagger said. It was SO weird. Ian was used to seeing his teachers

114

as just teachers, incapable of humour and always trying to force some fact or other into his brain. It felt really odd to see them smiling and relaxing.

"You really must try our spa here at Leviathan Hall," said Mr Grimble.

"Oh, I love spas," said Ms Husk. "They're so relaxing."

Mr Jagger rubbed the back of his neck.

"I must say, that certainly sounds good after such a long day."

Ian saw a smile creep across Mr Grimble's face. The way his tongue flicked out from between his lips made Ian feel nervous. Like he was watching a snake eyeing up a mouse.

"Well, why don't I take you to the spa after we've eaten?" Mr Grimble said. "A sauna and a massage will be the perfect way to unwind."

Ms Husk smiled at the idea, picked up her spoon and began tapping her glass. She stood up and the dining room fell silent.

"I would like to say a very big thank you to Mr Grimble and everyone at Leviathan Hall for making us feel so welcome."

Ian could hear the hooded waiters moaning softly in the candle-lit gloom.

"Now, we have an early start tomorrow for a morning of exciting-sounding activities," Ms Husk continued. "So, as it is getting so late, I want everyone up in their bedrooms after dinner."

A good-natured groan went up from the Dreary Inkling pupils.

"I'll pass around the roommates sheet now.

Take a look at who you're sharing with and pass the sheet on."

Ms Husk sat down and handed the piece of paper to Ian. He looked at it but couldn't see his name.

"Er, sorry, Ms Husk," he said. "I'm not on this list."

Ms Husk turned and looked at him.

"Really, er..." she said, peering at the name badge he was still wearing.

"It's Ian," sighed Ian.

"Er, Ian, of course," said Ms Husk. "I was sure I'd put everyone in a room."

She examined the paper for a minute.

"Well, that's most peculiar. I don't know what to say." She paused. "Can you help, Mr Grimble?"

Mr Grimble took the paper from Ms Husk.

"I believe that I might have a solution," he said.

But before Mr Grimble uttered another word, there was a sudden shriek from across the table. Hattie Lavernock was jumping up and down in excitement and holding something in the air.

"I found the finger," she yelled.

"Me too," yelled Eddie Splott. "I found one. I win." He looked at the finger that was covered in soup then licked it clean.

"Well done," said Mr Grimble. "If you just hand the fingers to Keith, you can both feed Daisy in the morning."

Ian watched as one of the hooded staff shuffled over to Hattie and Eddie and took the fingers from them both. The sight of them turned Ian's stomach. They didn't look like they were made of plastic; they looked like real fingers. Well, greeny-grey-coloured fingers with bits of skin missing. After the hooded waiter scurried away, Mr Grimble turned back towards Ms Husk.

"I believe we were discussing a solution to the bedroom problem," he said, looking at the

119

roommates list again. "Well, there might be space in room 13. Why don't I sort this out while you and your colleagues go to our lovely spa?"

He handed the list back to Ms Husk for her approval.

"Room 13?" said Ms Husk. "That's where Beano and Haroun are sleeping. Is there another bed in there?"

Mr Grimble fixed Ian with a stare that sent a chill down his spine.

"Sort of," he smiled.

# A BED WITH HOT AND COLD RUNNING WATER

Mr Grimble lit a single candle in the corner of Beano and Haroun's bathroom. The candle spluttered into life, eking a pale light into the room.

"Here you go," said Mr Grimble, throwing a pillow and blanket into the cracked bath. "You can sleep in there."

"In there?" said Ian, as a woodlouse scurried out from under a small bar of soap and headed for the plughole.

Mr Grimble nodded. "In there."

"I can't sleep in there," said Ian, peering into the bath. "It's unhygienic."

"It's perfectly hygienic," said Mr Grimble. "Why,

what could be more hygienic than sleeping in a bath? And think of the time you'll save in the morning. You'll be able to wake up and shower at the same time."

Mr Grimble smiled as he pulled a squashed foil-wrapped mint from his pocket and threw it on the wafer-thin pillow that lay scrunched up and unwelcoming in the hard, cracked bathtub.

"Now, if there's nothing else, I'll be on my way."

Ian couldn't think of anything to say so Mr Grimble shuffled out of the bathroom, shutting the door behind him. There was a sour, familiar odour about Mr Grimble that frightened Ian, although he wasn't sure why. Remington Furious III appeared in a puff of smoke wearing a full-length silk nightshirt and hat.

123

"A BATH?" he said. "YOU'VE GOT TO SLEEP IN A BATH?"

Ian sighed and listened to the laughter coming from inside the main bedroom. He opened the door a crack and saw Beano and Haroun jumping from bed to bed, whacking each other with pillows as hard as they could. Feathers were flying everywhere as the pair bounced and laughed until they were nearly crying.

"GREAT FUN!" roared Remington Furious III. "Go on, Ian, get stuck in."

Ian sat down on the toilet seat.

"I don't know," he said. "They might not want me to play with them."

But no sooner had the words left his lips than Haroun burst into the bathroom in a cloud of feathers and clonked him on the head.

"Quick, Ian!" he yelled, laughing and flinging his pillow around his head. "We're having a pillow fight. Beano is Joyce Crumble and she's trying to get our biscuits and we've got to stop her before she gets all the biscuits in the world. Come on!"

Then he dashed out of the bathroom and back into the bedroom.

"You heard him!" bellowed Remington Furious III. "Get pillowing! Stop that dastardly shoctopus!"

Ian grabbed his only-slightly-soggy pillow from the bath, whirled it around his head and whooped out of the bathroom.

"Take that, Joyce Crumble!" he laughed. "You'll never get our biscuits!"

As Ian battled against Beano and Haroun, then

125

joined forces with Haroun to attack Beano, then forged a tentative truce with Beano to campaign against Haroun, he didn't notice Remington Furious III, watching from on top of the wardrobe, beaming a big smile from ear-to-ear.

# BACKWARDS TROUSERS

Once everyone had gone to bed, Ian lay happily

in his bath and pulled his blanket around his ears.

After the great pillow fight, Beano had shared out

some of his snacks and the three boys had eaten

and laughed and talked about their best kills on

TIME VACUUM. Ian smiled and stretched out,

letting cold water from the tap drip onto his feet.

He wondered what would happen if he shoved

his big toe into the tap and got it stuck and he had

127

to stay in the bath for ever.

"The first thing we'd do would be to put the bath on a skateboard," said Remington Furious III, who was lying on the ceiling and was also considering the stuck-toe problem. "That way, you'd be able to push yourself around with a broom."

Ian thought for a moment.

"What about my pyjamas?" he said. "I'd have to change out of them to go to school but I wouldn't be able to get my bottoms off over the taps."

Remington Furious III dropped down from the ceiling onto the floor.

"Why we'd fashion you some backwards trousers, of course," he said, like it was the most normal thing in the world. "Trousers that you could take off over your head, like a jumper."

128

Ian looked at him.

"What? How would that work?"

Remington Furious III pondered the practicalities of backwards trousers.

"Well, we'll let the design team worry about the details," he said. "I'm more of an ideas man."

Ian chuckled at the thought of backwards trousers and was just contemplating the idea of backwards underpants, when he heard a noise.

129

CREEEEEEEEEEAAAAKKKKKKKKKK.

"WHAT WAS THAT?" yelled Remington Furious III.

Ian held his breath. The sound had come from somewhere deep within Leviathan Hall. He listened carefully but everything was quiet again.

"It's an old house," he whispered. "Old houses make weird noises. It's probably nothing."

He looked at his watch. It was 1.15 a.m. This was later than Ian had ever stayed up in his whole entire life.

Remington Furious III was now crouching on top of the toilet cistern.

"What if it isn't nothing?" he said, in a quiet, frightened sort of voice. "What if it's ghosts, or vampires, or werewolves, or zombies, or

130

mutant zombies?"

"Mutant zombies?" said Ian.

Remington Furious III jumped up and scanned the room nervously.

"MUTANT ZOMBIES?" he yelled. "WHERE?"

Ian climbed out of the bath.

"There aren't any ghosts or monsters or mutant zombies," he said, in a voice that sounded more confident than he felt. "But there is something weird about this place."

He walked over to his suitcase and took out his slippers.

"Maybe we should have a look around," he said. "You know, while everyone's asleep."

Ian walked out of the bathroom and into Haroun and Beano's bedroom. It was dark but

131

the moon outside gave just enough light for him to see where he was going.

"Shall we wake them?" said Remington Furious III. "Get them to come with us?"

Ian put on his slippers and looked at Beano and Haroun snoring softly in their beds.

"Nah," he whispered, grabbing the torch that he'd packed earlier. "They're just starting to like me. I don't want to risk them thinking I'm weird for hearing things and creeping around in the dark. Let them sleep. Come on, let's go."

Outside the bedroom door, Ian flicked on his torch and shone it down the hallway. He caught a glimpse of Remington Furious III, who had changed into his late-night safety poncho and mirrored cowboy boots.

"So where do we go?" said Remington Furious III.

In the pool of torchlight, Ian could see some doors down the corridor. He was just about to suggest checking them out, when he heard a noise. Actually, to be more precise, he heard two noises. A loud thump, like something big had fallen onto the floor, followed by another long CREEEEEEEEAAAAKKKKKK. And the noises were all coming from down the corridor, where his torch was shining.

Ian and Remington Furious III looked at each other for a split second and then ran. They didn't know where they were running, they just wanted to get as far away from the thumping as they could. The corridor turned left and right, this way and that and by the time he stopped running Ian

133

had absolutely no idea where he was.

He leaned against the wall of the corridor and tried to catch his breath.

Remington Furious III held up two carrots to his eyes, like binoculars, and looked back down the corridor.

"What are you doing?" whispered Ian.

"Carrots help you see in the dark," said Remington Furious III.

"You have to eat them," whispered Ian.

Remington Furious III put down his carrot binoculars and looked at Ian.

"You have to eat your eyes?" he said.

Ian sighed.

"No, you have to eat the carrots."

Remington Furious III looked at the carrots in his hands.

"What? Eat these?" he said throwing them onto the floor in disgust. "That's revolting."

As Ian stood in the darkness, waiting to see if the noise happened again, he noticed a faint, flickering, yellowy glow coming from around the corner. Ian held his breath, trying not to make a single sound. He clicked off his torch and as slowly and quietly as he could, edged his way down the corridor to take a closer look. Despite a feeling of terror rising in his body, Ian peered around the corner and saw Mr Grimble about ten metres away. He was holding a candelabra in his gloved hand and was talking to someone hidden in the shadows.

"We have just moved her, m'lady," said Mr Grimble.

"Good," rasped a horrible voice. "There are others to move tonight?"

Ian saw Mr Grimble nod.

"Yes, m'lady. Two more tonight. If all goes well, we shall move the others on the morrow."

"Excellent, Grimble, my plan is coming together perfectly," rasped the horrible voice. "By the weekend, the world will be mine. Nothing can stop me."

Mr Grimble and the figure began walking down the corridor, heading straight for Ian. He flinched with shock and took a step backwards onto a squeaky floorboard.

SQQQQUUUUEEEEEAAAKKKKKKKKKKK.

Mr Grimble and the other figure stopped walking.

"Who's there?" barked Mr Grimble.

Before Ian had a chance to do anything, Mr Grimble held up the candelabra, throwing its flickering light onto Ian's peeping face.

"Er, it's just me," said Ian, stepping out from around the corner.

"Well, well, well," said a woman, emerging out of the shadows. "And what do we have here?"

As Ian watched the woman move slowly into the light, a small gasp escaped his lips. The woman was wearing a flowing black lacy dress that reminded Ian of some boring historical drama that his mum watched on TV. Her hair was long and curly and so many different shades of grey that it looked like dirty snow stuck in a drain. But what truly shocked Ian was the woman's face. It was hard and smooth, like stone, and looked like the sort of face that only thought nasty things from the time it got up in the morning until the time it went to bed. And right in the middle of this severe, mean face were the sourest green eyes Ian had ever seen.

"I-I'm Ian," he stuttered. "Ian Iansson."

Ian couldn't stop looking at those terrible green eyes. They were like puddles of deadly radioactive waste and Ian felt like he was falling into them.

"Well, good evening, Ian Iansson," said the woman, with a voice so gravelly it could have been used to cover roads. "My name is Gertrude Leviathan."

Ian couldn't be certain but he thought he saw her green eyes glowing when she talked. He suddenly felt very, very cold.

Mr Grimble stalked over to where Ian was standing.

"What did you hear?" he snapped.

"Er, n-nothing," stammered Ian. "I just got here."

Gertrude Leviathan edged closer to Ian.

140

"What are you doing out of your room?" she said.

Ian wanted to back away but he couldn't move.

"I couldn't sleep," he said.

"The boy couldn't sleep, Mr Grimble. Perhaps you could help him?"

Mr Grimble stared hard at Ian and an awful smile flickered across his face.

"Of course, m'lady," he said, still staring at Ian. "Let's get you back into your room and tucked up in bed."

"In bath," said Ian.

"Oh, yes," said Mr Grimble. "Let's get you tucked up in bath."

141

# WEDNESDAY

# DARK MAGIC
# (YUM)

Ian sat cross-legged on the floor of the bedroom and listened as Haroun and Beano nattered away about TIME VACUUM.

"So, the other day, I had been dropped into Porkchop Vicarage and I found some legendary Glug Juice," said Haroun, looking at himself in the mirror.

Beano looked up from the comic he was reading, on his bed.

143

"What skin did you use?"

Haroun rubbed some wax into his thick, luxurious mane of hair.

"Junkhound Raider," he said.

"No way," said Beano. "That's really rare."

Haroun smiled.

"I know," he said, slicking his hair into a huge spike. "What's your best skin, Ian?"

But Ian wasn't listening. He was too busy thinking about what he'd seen the night before. He remembered hearing the strange noise and going to investigate. And he definitely remembered meeting Gertrude Leviathan with her cold, green eyes. But he had no memory of getting back to his room and when he'd woken up it was morning and he was in the cracked bath covered with

144

dozens of foil-wrapped mints.

"Did either of you hear anything in the night?" he said. "Anything weird, I mean."

Beano got off the bed and walked over to his suitcase.

"Nope," he said, rummaging around inside.

Haroun shook his head.

"Me neither," he said.

Ian looked around, like he was trying to make sure that no one could overhear him.

"I heard something," he said. "A sort of creaking sound only with lots of dragging and moaning too."

"Weird," said Beano, still rummaging in his suitcase.

Ian nodded.

145

"Then I saw Mr Grimble and Gertrude Leviathan."

BONG!

The breakfast gong sounded.

"Gertrude Leviathan?" said Haroun. "What's she like?"

"Well, she looks really, really old, like she must be well over forty," said Ian.

"That IS old," said Beano.

"Yeah, but that's not the weird thing," continued Ian. "They were talking about moving people, and Gertrude Leviathan said she was going to 'own the world' by the weekend."

"It's Dark Magic," said Beano.

"What?" said Ian. "You think so? I mean she was creepy and all but dark magic? Really?"

146

"No," said Beano. "Dark Magic."

He held out a box of chocolates that said *Dark Magic - the darkest chocolate with a creamy toffee centre.*

"I thought you might like a pre-breakfast choccie," he said.

The breakfast gong sounded again.

Ian and Haroun each took a Dark Magic from the box and the three boys made their way out of the room.

"Maybe you were sleepwalking last night," said Beano, as they headed down the corridor. "You might have been dreaming."

Ian had considered this possibility. In fact, when he woke up, his first thought had been that he had dreamed the whole thing. But as he walked

147

through Leviathan Hall, and into the dining room, Ian knew that it hadn't been a dream at all. A horribly familiar woman was standing by the dining table, waiting for them. A woman with hair the colour of dirty snow, and eyes like puddles of radioactive waste.

"Ah, young gentlemen, thank you for joining us," rasped Gertrude Leviathan.

Ian, Haroun and Beano found three empty seats and sat down as Gertrude Leviathan walked around the table. At least, Ian assumed she was walking, but her feet were hidden by the bottom of a long, black dress, which made it look like she was floating.

"Welcome to you all," she said, her deep throaty voice echoing off the walls. "I trust you had a good night's sleep."

An unsettling, eerie feeling wrapped itself around Ian. He turned to Beano, who was buttering some toast.

"She's the woman I saw last night," he whispered. "Don't you think there's something really weird about this place? I've had the strangest feeling since we got here. It's like we're being watched all the time or something."

But Beano wasn't listening. He was too busy sniffing a pot of gloopy beetroot marmalade.

"Leviathan Hall is my home," Gertrude Leviathan continued, fiddling with a large green amulet that hung from her neck. "It has been in

150

my family ever since it was acquired by my great, great, great, great, great, great, great, great, great, great, great, great, great, great, great, great, great, great, great, great, great, great, great, great great grandfather, Augustus Leviathan. The story goes that he won Leviathan Hall from the devil himself."

A gasp went up around the dining hall.

"Yes," she said. "'Twas a most unusual game of I-Spy."

Gertrude Leviathan paused for a moment.

"Now, I want you all to have a good breakfast," she said, rubbing her smooth cheeks. "You must be ready for all the exciting activities we have planned for you today. I understand that some of you will be feeding Daisy."

Hattie and Eddie looked at each other and smiled.

"Well, the rest of you children will be split into two groups," Gertrude Leviathan continued. "Mr Grimble will take some of you to learn some woodcrafting skills and the rest will come with me on a thrilling scavenger hunt."

Brianna Grimditch put up her hand.

"Where's Ms Husk?" she said.

Gertrude Leviathan stared at Brianna down the end of her long, pointy nose.

"Why, you're a curious little one, aren't you?" she said, smiling at Brianna. Or, at least, she tried to smile at Brianna but her face sort of shuddered at the effort. Ian thought it made Gertrude Leviathan look as though her skin wasn't big enough to stretch across her face.

"I'm afraid that Ms Husk was taken ill yesterday evening, during her session at the Leviathan spa, and was moved to our infirmary. I checked on her this morning and am happy to report that she looked much better. She wanted me to tell you that, whilst she is too weak to join in today's fun, she will see you all tomorrow and that absolutely nothing unusual or sinister has happened to her."

Ian felt the eerie, unsettling feeling again. Tom Boosbeck put up his hand. Gertrude Leviathan fixed him with her green-eyed stare.

"What now?" she barked.

"I just wondered where Mr Jagger and Ms Fluther-Smack are?" asked Tom.

Gertrude Leviathan's eyes narrowed.

153

"They were also taken ill in the spa and are also in the infirmary," she said in a growl, staring straight at Tom. "They are also too weak to join in today's fun but also wanted to reassure you that there is also absolutely nothing for you to worry about."

"Do you believe her?" Ian whispered to Haroun and Beano. "All three teachers ill? At the same time? Doesn't that sound a bit weird? And what is up with her face?"

Ian suddenly felt the air chill around him and saw a look of horror flash across Haroun's face as he saw something over Ian's shoulder.

"Oh, I'm sorry to interrupt your conversation," rasped Gertrude Leviathan, who was standing behind Ian. "But I thought I heard someone utter

154

my name. Did you wish to say something, boy?"

The dining room fell silent.

"Er, no," said Ian, quietly.

Gertrude Leviathan allowed the silence to fester for a moment, her eyes burning into Ian like she was examining the inside of his soul.

"I'm glad to hear it," she said eventually. "Now, while the rest of us eat, Mr Grimble will be taking the two lucky winners of yesterday's competition to go and feed Daisy. After all, she needs her breakfast too."

She walked over to where Mr Grimble was

155

standing and whispered something to him. Ian watched him nod, then walk over to where Hattie and Eddie were sitting and lead them out of the dining room. Ian snuck a look at Gertrude Leviathan, who was rubbing her green amulet between her fingers. For a second, it looked like the amulet started to glow. It was the exact same green glow that Ian had seen at the grimy window the day before.

# MISSING KIDS AND A MISSING LEG

Ian waited at the foot of the staircase in the grand entrance hall. He, and half the class, had been told by Gertrude Leviathan to wait for Mr Grimble. They would be in his group for their first exciting woodcrafting activity. Ian watched his classmates. Drishya Samode hooked arms with Grace Smeaton and Betty Gabalfa, while Commodore Sinclair, Elton Gweek and Tom Boosbeck stood chatting and laughing together.

"I wish Beano and Haroun were coming with us," said Remington Furious III, brushing the front of his bright pink lumberjack outfit. "I was just beginning to like them. Well, apart from the snoring."

Ian turned and glanced down the corridor. In the distance, he noticed one of the hooded waiters, carrying a large tray of dirty plates.

"I know," he said, looking back at Tom Boosbeck, who was licking his finger and sticking it in Elton Gweek's ear. "We said we'll all sit together at lunch when they get back from their scavenger hunt though."

There was a sudden clatter from down the corridor. Ian turned and saw the waiter had fallen over, dropping the tray of plates all over the floor.

158

Next, he saw Mr Grimble emerge from a doorway and say something angrily. Ian couldn't make it out, as they were too far away, but eventually Mr Grimble helped the waiter to their feet. Well actually, he seemed to help the waiter to their foot.

"Oh my god," said Ian, as he watched Mr Grimble pick up something long and limb-like. "It looks like their leg's fallen off."

Remington Furious III sniffed.

"Maybe it's a false leg or something," he said.

Ian continued to watch the waiter as they hopped through a door and disappeared. Mr Grimble threw the leg after them.

159

"He's not very nice to the staff, is he?" said Ian, as Mr Grimble prowled down the corridor towards him.

Ian stepped back as Mr Grimble swept into the entrance hall, looking flustered, and addressed the group. His waxy skin had a damp sheen to it.

"Well, woodcrafters," he said, trying to smooth down his wisp of hair. "You're going to be making something very interesting this morning."

There was a murmur of excitement. Drishya put up her hand.

"Are we waiting for Hattie and Eddie?" she said. "They're both in our group."

Mr Grimble paused for a moment. One eye twitched.

"Er, no, both Hattie and Eddie, were, er, taken
ill just after they fed Daisy. Most peculiar and
sudden. They must, er, have the same thing that
your teachers have."

Ian looked at Remington Furious III. None of
this was making sense to him.

"Taken ill?" he whispered.
"How did that happen?"

"Maybe Daisy had
a cold?" suggested
Remington Furious
III. "Or maybe the
dead rat they fed her
wasn't dead and had
some weird mutant rat
disease and it bit Hattie

and Eddie and that's how they fell ill."

Ian wasn't convinced.

"But you mustn't worry," continued Mr Grimble, his mouth stretching into a crooked smile that revealed his horrible teeth. "I'm sure they'll be much better before too long."

And with that, he opened the imposing front doors and headed outside.

"Come along," he said.

Ian paused as the rest of the class followed Mr Grimble.

"What if Gertrude Leviathan and Mr Grimble are up to something?" he said. "I mean, that's a lot of people who have just fallen ill, isn't it?"

Remington Furious III nodded.

"And the Leviathan staff are really weird too."

162

Remington Furious III nodded again.

"There's something strange going on here," said Ian, following the rest of the class into the early morning sunshine. "We need to have a look around on our own, without Gertrude Leviathan or Mr Grimble breathing down our necks."

163

THE LEVIATHAN FAMILY
ReCREATIONAL PICNIC
AND SACRIFICE AREA

Ian ran to catch up with the rest of the group as they marched across the grass opposite Leviathan Hall. An ancient stone signpost pointed towards the back of the lawn. It had a tatty piece of card taped over the front of it, with the words scrawled in black marker pen.

The woods
of Tranquillity
THIS WAY

"They don't look very tranquil," whispered Ian, as the lawn eventually gave way to a thicket of gnarled, leafless trees.

"No, they don't," said Remington Furious III. "They look the opposite of tranquil. Totally untranquillitated, if you ask me."

Mr Grimble led everyone along a stony path and deeper into the Woods of Tranquillity. The further down the path they walked, the darker and colder the wood became. Ian undid his hoodie from around his waist and put it on, zipping it up tight. Remington Furious III put on his knitted pink onesie and matching balaclava.

It was getting so gloomy that Ian had to turn his torch on. The dark and the eerie quiet of the woods were making everyone a bit frightened.

Especially when Tom Boosbeck started making howling wolf noises, which scared Elton Gweek so much that he screamed and fell into a bush. Eventually though, the trees opened out into a bright, sunlit clearing. Mr Grimble stopped by a large pile of wood and nails.

"Here we are, right in the very heart of the Woods of Tranquillity," he said, just as a cloud of bats flapped out of the trees and everyone started screaming.

"Many years ago," continued Mr Grimble, once the bats had gone and everyone had calmed down, "this clearing was thought of as a place of great and mysterious power. There are stories of sacrifices happening right here in the name of the darkest and most evil magic."

Betty Gabalfa looked nervously around the clearing.

"E-evil magic? S-sacrifices?" she said. "H-here?"

Mr Grimble smiled.

"Do not worry, they were just tales to scare children in the dark. There will be no sacrifices, I promise."

He looked at his watch and his tongue flicked out of his mouth for a second. "Well, not today."

Betty laughed uncertainly.

"Now, later this evening, we have planned to have a bonfire and a marshmallow roast right here in the woods," he said.

Everyone cheered at the news.

"But because of a strange local historical law,

167

we need a special marshmallow-roasting safety platform. And so, your woodcrafting exercise this morning is to help build it."

Ian thought for a moment, using his incredible imagination to try and come up with a reason why there would need to be a special platform built, just to roast marshmallows. But he couldn't.

"We have all the materials for you," said Mr Grimble, clapping his hands twice. "As well as an army of helpers."

Dozens of hooded staff moaned and staggered from out of the trees and began picking up tools and bits of wood.

"Excellent," said Mr Grimble. "Let us begin."

As the morning wore on, the children and the hooded Leviathan Hall staff worked hard, hammering and sawing and building the marshmallow-roasting safety platform. One of the staff members shuffled over to Mr Grimble.

"Me no have hammer," he said.

"What do you mean you haven't got a hammer?" said Mr Grimble, irritably. "I definitely brought enough hammers for everyone."

The hooded staff member shrugged.

"Me no have hammer," they repeated.

Mr Grimble tutted and sighed.

"Well, there are lots of hard objects around that you can use to bash a nail in," he said, looking around the clearing. "Honestly, do I have to think of every little thing? Why can't you just use your head for a change?"

"Okay," said the staff member. "Me use head."

169

Then they walked back to where they had been working and began trying to hammer a nail in by smashing their face against it. Mr Grimble rolled his eyes.

Eventually, the marshmallow-roasting safety platform began to take shape. Although, it wasn't quite the sort of shape Ian had imagined.

"It's a bit funny looking, isn't it?" he whispered.

"Mmmm," agreed Remington Furious III.

"It's a bit, erm, oh I don't know, how would you describe it?"

"Cage-y?" offered Ian, holding onto one of the thick wooden bars that lined the walls of the platform.

Remington Furious III stopped for a moment

and considered the marshmallow-roasting safety platform.

"Yes," he nodded. "That's exactly it. It is a bit cage-y."

Mr Grimble clapped his hands together to get everyone's attention.

"Excellent work, children," he said, holding up some chains and padlocks. "Now, I need some volunteers to start attaching these to the platform. Anyone?"

Ian put his hand up.

"Yes?" said Mr Grimble. "Are you volunteering?"

"Erm, well, actually I have a question," said Ian. "I was just wondering why we need chains and padlocks on a marshmallow-roasting safety platform?"

Mr Grimble levelled a ferocious grade eight, black-belt stare at Ian.

"The chains and padlocks are for decoration," he said. "And also for health and safety reasons."

Ian looked at Mr Grimble and then at Remington Furious III.

"I don't like this," he whispered. "First chance we get, we need to do some investigating."

A first chance didn't take long to materialize. After another half an hour of building, Mr Grimble went to check on how the scavenger hunt was going. Once Ian was sure he'd gone, he started hopping from foot-to-foot and jigged over to a hooded staff member.

"Er, I need to go to the toilet," he said.

The staff member, who had been gluing sharp

173

wooden spikes onto the top of the platform bars, stood up. Ian heard a moan that sounded like "HALL" coming from somewhere inside their hood.

"Back at the hall?" he said.

The hooded figure nodded and returned to their gluing.

Ian hopped out of the clearing and, as soon as he was clear of any prying hooded eyes, ran back through the Woods of Tranquillity and onto the large lawn. He sprinted past the ancient signpost so quickly that he didn't notice that the piece of tatty card with the words WOODS OF TRANQUILLITY scrawled on it had fallen off. The sign now read:

Leviathan Family
Recreational Picnic
and Sacrifice Area
This Way →

When Ian reached Leviathan Hall, the place was deserted. He peeked inside the dining room, where places were set for lunch but no one was around at all. He walked back into the entrance hall.

"I think I know where we should try first," he said. "The door with the dragon handle."

Remington Furious III adjusted his leather-tasselled deerstalker hat.

"But that's the one that Mr Grimble said you should never go through," he said.

Ian nodded.

"In fact," continued Remington Furious III. "He said you should never ever, ever, ever, ever go through that door."

"I know," said Ian, walking down the corridor.

"It was weird that he made such a fuss. I mean it's only a toilet, isn't it?"

Remington Furious III didn't answer, he just floated alongside Ian until they reached the door with the dragon handle.

"Look at its eyes!" gasped Ian.

He hadn't spotted it when he'd first seen the handle but the dragon's eyes were made of two small green stones.

"They're exactly the same colour as Gertrude Leviathan's amulet," said Remington Furious III. "You sure you want to do this?"

Ian took a deep breath and nodded. Then, grasping the dragon's head in his hand, he carefully turned the handle and the door yawned open.

176

# GERTRUDE LEVIATHAN

Behind the open dragon's-eyes door, there wasn't any sign of a toilet, decorated or undecorated. Instead, Ian could just about see a dark corridor stretching out in front of him. He shone his torch and stepped through the doorway. The air in the passage was clammy and Ian could hear his footsteps echo off the stone walls.

He shone the light down to the end of the corridor and saw a large wooden door, with the

177

words LEVIATHAN LIBRARY written on it.

As Ian walked up to the door, a large millipede scuttled out of the keyhole. Ian fought the urge to scream and run away. Once the millipede had scurried off, Ian pushed the door and it slowly creaked open.

"I don't like it," said Remington Furious III. "It's so creepy."

"I know," said Ian, with a deep breath. "But this might be our only chance to have a proper look around."

He carefully shone the torch in front of him and took a step inside.

In the torchlight, Ian could see rows and rows of large shelves, each filled with old, leather-bound books, that mostly seemed to be about

178

magic. There were books with titles like *The Good Guide to Evil Magic*, and *Which Witch: The World's Most Famous Witches and Wizards*, and *Student Spells: Emergency Magic on a Budget*.

Ian walked past shelf after shelf until he came to a table that had some candles surrounding a large book with a golden cover. He shone the torch on the book to take a closer look. It said:

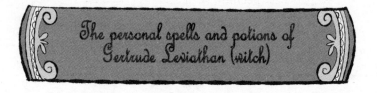

The personal spells and potions of
Gertrude Leviathan (witch)

"Witch?" he said, his heart suddenly beating very fast.

Ian opened the book and slowly turned to the first page.

180

<u>Friday, August 14th, 1908</u>

Today was such an exciting day because it was my sixteenth birthday and I was finally allowed to attempt my first ever spell. It was one that I found in an ancient book of magic that Aunt Vestibule gave me as a present. I was supposed to make gold coins appear from a bag, but I must have done something really wrong, because I ended up making green slime appear instead. It made such a mess. Mummy was really cross. Will try again tomorrow.

"Rubbish at spells?" said Ian. "Ancient book of magic? Sixteen? I don't understand."

He looked at the date of the diary entry and

looked at Remington Furious III.

"It must be a different Gertrude Leviathan," he said, turning to another random page. "Otherwise she'd be—" Ian tried to do the maths. "Really, really old."

<u>Tuesday, November 10th, 1908</u>

Another terrible failure. No matter how hard I try, I just can't seem to master the easiest spells. Today, I tried to turn a frog into a prince but I ended up turning a frog into a slightly bigger frog but with a human nose. Mummy got really angry when I couldn't do it and told me I'd never be a proper witch if I couldn't do these really basic spells. Went to bed crying. Aunt Vestibule cheered me up though. She thinks I should try doing only evil spells. She says that different people are good at different things. She gave me a green amulet. She told me that if I wear it, the stone will help channel my powers. I shall try again tomorrow.

Ian turned the page.

Wednesday, November 11th, 1908
Success! I performed a level three evil spell perfectly. I created my own evil servant out of a lump of my earwax. I will give him the name of my most hated schoolteacher. It will amuse me to give orders to something with the name Mr Grimble. The amulet began glowing as I performed the spell, I could feel its power flow through me

and shoot out of my fingers. I have decided that when I leave school I will become the greatest evil witch the world has ever seen.

The book suddenly felt very heavy in Ian's hands.

"I-I don't believe it," he said, letting it fall to his side. "It *is* the same Gertrude Leviathan and she's a witch."

A loose leaf of paper fell out of the back of the book. Ian picked it up and shone the torchlight onto it.

"It's some sort of list," he said, scanning it.

His eyes widened as he read the final entry.

"Look at this," he said. "We have to get some help."

184

# FROM THE DESK OF
## GERTRUDE LEVIATHAN
# TO DO

- A "BIG" SHOP AT WIDDLE (get extra teabags)

- TAKE POINTY BLACK HAT TO DRYCLEANERS

- CREATE EVIL ZOMBIE ARMY

## GERTRUDE LEVIATHAN'S EVIL PLANNING OFFICE

Ian paced the floor while Remington Furious III floated above him.

"Okay," said Ian, not looking at all like he thought things were okay. "Okay. Okay. Okay. Okay. Okay. Okay. Okay."

He paused.

"Okay."

"Okay?" asked Remington Furious III.

Ian nodded.

186

"Okay," he said again. "Is there any other, non-creepy reason why an ancient witch would want to create a zombie army? Maybe it's code for something?"

"Code for what?" said Remington Furious III.

"I don't know," said Ian, panic rising in his voice. "'Create evil zombie army' could really mean 'put together surprise birthday party', couldn't it?"

He looked nervously at Remington Furious III and began flicking through Gertrude Leviathan's dairy again.

Thursday, February 29th, 1968

I grow weary of performing evil magic. For the last sixty years I have summoned demons from

187

fiery pits, cast curses and hexes on friends and foe, and even had three Christmas number ones in a row. But I tire of such meaningless trickery. My evil powers are destined for something greater than this. I have invited dear Aunt Vestibule over tomorrow for some delicious dragon's mucus and entrails. She will know what to do, I am certain.

Friday, March 1st, 1968

At last, I have found something worthy of my evil skills. Aunt Vestibule found an ancient manuscript for something called the Great Curse. Its power is immense and with it so will mine become. But I must be patient. The Great Curse is written in an ancient magic language that only

188

three people in the whole world understand. It will take many decades of learning before I will understand it fully. I will dedicate my life to this and shall not write another diary entry until I am ready.

Ian looked at the next page, then at Remington Furious III.

"She didn't write anything again until about a month ago," he said.

Saturday, 14th May

At last, after many years of learning, I am ready to perform the Great Curse. I have translated the manuscript and have everything I need to create my zombie army. The Leviathan family is all here

189

at the Hall, even Uncle Keith and Great-Aunt Bernard have made the long trip from the place they call Wolverhampton. All are ready to form my army of the undead. They will wreak terror on the world as they roam from town to town and city to city, feasting on the brains of ordinary people, until everyone in the world is a zombie, and under my control. As dear Uncle Nestor said, "There's nothing like a good family activity to bring everyone together."

"She wants to control the world," muttered Ian, looking at the next page.

Sunday, 15th May
We have missed our opportunity! Everything was ready but something went very badly wrong

with the curse. Grimble used beetroot juice instead of bat's blood. He has turned my family into pathetic vegetarian zombies that just wander around with stupid smiles plastered on their rotten faces. The Great Curse must be performed under a full moon so we shall have to wait for another month to pass before we can try again. Grimble says he will organize another group of people to cast the curse on. I shall take the opportunity to have a restorative sleep in my Tomb of Rejuvenations. All this evil makes me very tired.

"Okay," said Ian. "So the words 'create a zombie army' actually do mean create a zombie army.

191

We need to find Ms Husk and the other teachers and warn them."

Suddenly, they heard a huge crashing sound.

"What was that?" said Remington Furious III.

Ian flicked off his torch and hid behind a bookshelf. He waited for a few moments not daring to even breathe. Finally, Remington Furious III floated over to where he was hiding.

"I think the noise came from over there," he whispered, pointing into the darkness in one corner of the library. Ian shone his torch and saw a small passageway.

"We should check it out."

"What?" said Remington Furious III. "We're in the house of an evil witch. Why would we want to check out the weird crashing noise?"

Ian got down on his hands and knees.

"Because we need to find the teachers and that's as good a place as anywhere to start looking," he said and began crawling over.

The passageway wasn't very long, and at the end of it, Ian could see a thin sliver of light creep out from underneath a door. He could feel his hands getting cold and clammy with sweat.

"Let's take a look," whispered Ian.

He crept over to the door and gently pushed it open. Remington Furious III floated over as Ian peered inside. The door led to a room lit by flickering candles. There was a big desk at one end, behind which Gertrude Leviathan was sitting. Ian crouched behind an enormous ornamental vase that was positioned just inside the door. He saw Gertrude Leviathan's green eyes flashing in the gloom.

"By the hairs of Lord Satan's armpits, why are you so clumsy!" she shrieked.

A hooded staff member was standing over an upturned tray of food, which had completely ruined the rug by the desk.

"I wanted a bite to eat," screeched Gertrude

194

Leviathan. "I did not want my beautiful office, where I hatch all my evil plans, to be redecorated with food."

"Me drop tray," said the staff member. "Me sorry."

"I know you dropped the tray, you snaggle-toothed gibface," said Gertrude Leviathan, pounding her fists on the desk with such evil fury that sparks of electricity flew out of them. A shock wave vibrated through the floor and was so ferocious that the staff member's hood was blown back.

From behind the shaking ornamental vase, Ian stared at the scene in front of him, scarcely able to believe what he was looking at. The staff member's face was human, yet not human. Their skin was a greeny-grey sort of colour, like the mould on the tangerine that he'd forgotten at the bottom of his school bag once. One of the staff member's eye sockets was empty, whilst the other eye was swollen and red and swivelling around wildly, never settling for a second.

"USELESS!" screamed Gertrude Leviathan, who gave the table another angry thump.

The vibrations shuddered through the floor again, this time knocking the staff member's head off their shoulders.

"My head come off," said the staff member's mouth, from the head that was bouncing around, still attached to its body by long strands of sinew and veins.

Ian watched from behind the vase, opening and closing his mouth like a terrified fish.

"I am so sick of you and all the other useless zombies," shouted Gertrude Leviathan, picking up a small bell from her desk and ringing it. "I shall be turning you all into statues after I perform the Great Curse."

"Z-zombies," whispered Ian. "They're the zombies she was talking about in her diary. The ones that went wrong."

"Well, that does explain the moaning and the body parts falling off," said Remington Furious III.

Mr Grimble appeared through a door on the other side of the room. Gertrude Leviathan turned towards him.

"Ah, Grimble, there you are," she snarled. "One of your staff has just ruined my rug and their head has fallen off. Get them out of here and get this mess cleaned up."

Mr Grimble looked at the spilled food, then at the headless zombie. His hair seemed to shake a little bit.

"A thousand apologies, m'lady," he said, ushering the zombie out of the door. "I shall see to it immediately."

As Mr Grimble was about to leave, Gertrude Leviathan stood up from the desk.

"Is the rest of our plan on schedule?"

"Oh, yes, m'lady," said Mr Grimble. "The moon will be full tonight and perfect for the Great Curse to begin."

"There will be no mistakes this time," snapped Gertrude Leviathan. "I do not want another useless army of zombies. I want proper, evil, brain-eaters. Got it?"

"Perfectly, m'lady," said Mr Grimble. "The children are just eating their lunch now. It has been laced with a sleeping draught. In a few

200

minutes they will all be asleep and ready to be moved. In a few hours you will have a ravenous, slobbering, brain-chomping army of zombies."

Gertrude Leviathan clapped her hands together.

"Oh goody," she said.

Behind the ornamental vase, Ian's face was stricken with terror. He quietly crawled back through the door and looked at Remington Furious III. Neither said a word. They knew that now was not a time for talking, it was a time for doing, and Ian knew exactly what he had to do. He had to save his whole class from being turned into brain-sucking zombies by a witch and someone made out of earwax. But in order to do it, he knew he needed to get some help.

# THE LAST HOPE

Ian raced back to the dining room as quickly as he could, his mind a whirl of zombies and curses and severed heads. When he got there he was so sweaty and hot that he took off his hoodie and tied it around his waist. Ian scanned the room, as his classmates were just finishing lunch. Everyone looked absolutely shattered. Drishya Samode's head nodded about as she desperately tried to keep her eyes open. Luna Axminster and Elton Gweek

were fast asleep, face down in their beetroot salad. And Commodore Sinclair was yawning and stretching and looked like he was about to turn in for the night, even though it was only quarter past one in the afternoon.

Ian quickly found Beano and Haroun and dashed over.

"Where have you been?" said Beano, food tumbling out of his yawning mouth.

"We've got to get out of here," said Ian. "We've got to get everyone out of here. You've all been drugged with some kind of super sleeping draught. Gertrude Leviathan wants to turn us all into zombies."

Haroun yawned and laughed.

"Zombies? Yeah, right," he said. "How's she going to do that then?"

Ian looked around and moved in closer to his friends.

"I'm not entirely sure," he said. "But it's true. It's going to happen tonight under a full moon. I went through the door that Grimble told us not to go through and there's this library and then I found a book and it was Gertrude Leviathan's diary and she's a w—"

But before Ian could get the word "witch" out of

his mouth, he felt a chill in the room and stopped what he was saying. Gertrude Leviathan and Mr Grimble had appeared in the doorway. Ian quickly sat down at the table next to Beano and Haroun.

"Children," growled Gertrude Leviathan. "Have you all had enough to eat?"

Ian watched everyone nod and smile and yawn. Gertrude Leviathan looked around the room, her mouth wanting to turn up into a smile but her clamped, tight skin not allowing her.

"Is everyone looking forward to the bonfire and marshmallow roasting later?" she said. "Because I am."

Some of Ian's class nodded. Mostly they all just yawned.

"Well, as you all seem so tired, then perhaps

205

everyone would like to go to their rooms for a lie-down before the real fun can begin?"

Ian looked at the horrific smile that spread across Gertrude Leviathan's face and then at his friends and classmates, their heads lolling, and he knew that he needed to camouflage himself by acting like he was really tired. He started pretend yawning.

"Come along then, children," said Gertrude Leviathan, her voice low and deep and full of danger. "Why don't you all go upstairs to your rooms?"

Haroun and Beano, like the rest of Ian's class, slowly staggered to their feet and began shuffling out of the dining room and towards the grand staircase. Ian did the same, making sure that he yawned a lot so he didn't look out of place.

"So tired," said Haroun.

"So very, very tired," agreed Beano.

Mr Grimble and Gertrude Leviathan were standing at the bottom of the staircase, watching everyone as they stumbled up towards their rooms. For a second, their attention was distracted when Drishya Samode stumbled and fell asleep halfway up the stairs.

"Quick," whispered Ian, grabbing Beano and Haroun and pulling them behind a large wing-backed armchair in the hallway.

"What are you doing?" said Beano.

"I want to go to bed," said Haroun.

"Sshhhh," hushed Ian, peeping out from behind the chair.

He watched and waited until the last of his classmates made their way, yawning, up the stairs. Gertrude Leviathan rubbed her hands.

"We will move our volunteers this evening," she said, walking up the stairs.

"Yes, m'lady," said Mr Grimble, following behind. "I don't foresee any problems."

"Excellent, Grimble, take your time. You have several hours before the full moon appears. I don't want any more mistakes. Inform me when everything is ready."

She stepped over Drishya, who was lying snoring on the stairs.

"Leave this one here if you like."

Once Ian was sure that Gertrude Leviathan and Mr Grimble had disappeared up the stairs, he jumped up from behind the chair.

"Right, let's go," he said. "Follow me."

He started walking across the entrance hall.

"We have to find Ms Husk and get her phone. She said we could use it in an emergency. Well, this is a flippin' emergency."

Remington Furious III appeared wearing his purple velvet travel-jumpsuit.

"They're not going to be much use, are they?" he said, pointing back at Beano and Haroun, who had fallen asleep behind the chair.

Ian rushed back over and began shaking Beano and slapping Haroun's face.

"Wake up! You've got to wake up! I need you!"

He turned and looked at Remington Furious III.

"What are we going to do?"

210

Remington Furious III pointed at the front door of Leviathan Hall.

"We can escape," he said. "This is your chance, Ian. You can run away."

Ian looked at the door. He knew he probably should go. That he could maybe get help from somewhere. But then he looked at his friends and he knew he couldn't leave them. All he had to do was get to Ms Husk's phone.

"I can't leave them," he said, kneeling over Haroun's snoozing body. "I just can't."

Remington Furious III edged towards the door.

"You can, Ian, you can. Leave them and follow me. Save yourself."

Ian stood up and stared at Remington Furious III. His fists were clenched, his jaw set, ready for

211

a fight, ready for action.

"No," he said. "I'm not leaving them. I'm not leaving anyone to that witch. We've got to find Ms Husk's phone and call for help."

Remington Furious III sighed.

"But we don't know where she is," he said. "How will we find her?"

Ian took a deep breath. He might only be a boy wearing a grey T-shirt, slightly too-small jeans, and his fourth-best pair of pants but he knew that it was time to show everyone who he really was.

"I don't know, but we've got to try, even if we have to look in every room in this whole place," he said. "Gertrude Leviathan is not going to turn any of us into zombies because we're going to stop her."

212

# A VERY
# PAINFUL LOOKING
# SPA TREATMENT

Ian clicked on his torch and he and Remington
Furious III set off through Leviathan Hall. They
moved quickly past the door with the dragon
handle and had just gone past Daisy's pool room
when Ian tripped over something.

"OW! What was that?"

He shone his torch onto the floor and saw a
zombie arm, with a hand attached, just lying there,
on its own. It was a horrible shade of green and

was so thin that it was practically just skin and bone.

"That is SO gross," said Ian, who found that, even though the sight of the disembodied limb made him feel sick, he just couldn't stop staring at it. There was something about the rotting and separated appendage that he found strangely hypnotic.

"Go on, touch it," said Remington Furious III. "What does it feel like?"

Slowly, Ian bent down, reached out his fingers and gently pushed on the flaky, green skin.

"It just feels all bony," he said, picking the arm up and waving it at Remington Furious III. "Hello there, I'm an arm."

Remington Furious III burst out laughing.

"Pleased to meet you," said Ian, holding the arm out towards Remington Furious III. "Would you like to shake my hand?"

Remington Furious III howled with laughter. But suddenly Ian started jumping up and down and shouting.

"It's moving!" he said. "It's alive!"

Without Ian doing anything, the zombie hand had flexed its fingers and began wiggling around. Ian tried to catch it but before he could, the hand walked up his arm and grabbed onto his shoulder, hard.

215

Ian pulled and pulled and pulled but it wouldn't come off. It had clamped itself on tight.

"Get it off me, get it off me," he shouted. But it was no good. The arm was stuck.

Ian stopped shouting and took several long, deep breaths to calm down.

"What's it doing?" he said eventually, looking at the zombie limb that was clinging happily to his shoulder.

Remington Furious III shrugged.

"Dunno," he said. "Maybe being an arm is all that it knows. Maybe it would rather be an upside-down arm on a human than lying on some cold, dirty floor."

A moaning sound echoed down the corridor and Ian could see flickering torchlight coming

216

from around the corner.

"It's a zombie," said Ian. "We need to hide."

"Quick, in here," said Remington Furious III, pointing to a door.

The moaning was getting louder and louder.

"It might be the zombie who lost their arm," whispered Ian.

Remington Furious III looked at Ian.

"Don't worry," he said. "I'm sure he's 'armless."

Ignoring Remington Furious III's terrible joke, Ian quickly undid his hoodie from around his waist and put it on, covering up the zombie arm. The moaning was getting closer. The zombie would be around the corner any moment.

"Come on," said Ian, opening the door and hurrying through.

217

Ian carefully closed the door behind him. He held his breath as the zombie shuffled past the door but, before long, the moaning began to get quieter.

Ian let out a big sigh of relief and wriggled his shoulder. The zombie arm was still attached and not showing any sign of letting go.

"Come on, let's find Ms Husk," he said, opening the door. "It's all clear."

Remington Furious III was waiting for him in the corridor.

"Where now?" he said.

Ian shone his torch down the corridor. There were doors on either side.

"Just try every door, one of them must be the infirmary," he said. "I'll do this side, you do the other side."

Remington Furious III looked at him.

"How am I supposed to do that?" he said. "I'm a figment of your imagination."

Ian cursed under his breath.

"Yes, sorry, I forgot," he said.

"I occupy no physical space of my own," continued Remington Furious III. "And I am, therefore, unable to open these, or any other, doors."

"Alright, alright," said Ian.

He wanted to tell Remington Furious III to be quiet, that he wasn't helping things at all and, at this moment in time, was of absolutely no use to Ian. But he didn't have to say anything because Remington Furious III was part of Ian and he knew. And so, he slowly disappeared and left

Ian, in the corridor, on his own. The colossal colossalness of what he had to do suddenly hit Ian like a runaway killer whale on skis. Not only was he in the creepiest house in the world and had to stop an evil witch from turning him, and all his classmates, into zombies. But he had to do it all by himself.

# YOU DON'T HAVE TO BE ZOMBIFIED TO WORK HERE, BUT IT HELPS

Ian gathered himself; he knew he didn't have any time to waste. He took a deep breath, raced down the corridor to the next door and slowly opened it. He shone his torch inside and saw that the room was empty except for a gigantic hole in the middle of the floor with a sign next to it that said, BOTTOMLESS PIT.

"Okay, no infirmary in here," he said to himself, shutting the door.

221

He rushed to the next door and opened that. The whole room was piled high with skulls and bones.

"Not in here, either," said Ian.

He shone his light down the corridor again and, this time, spotted a door that had the word PRIVATE written on it. Ian carefully walked up to it and slowly pushed it open. Dozens and dozens of swollen red eyes swivelled in his direction. The room was full of zombies, some drinking strange purple-coloured drinks, others playing cards around a big table. But all of them had stopped what they were doing and now stared at Ian. Ian felt panic rising in his body. He looked at a sign on the wall that read:

## YOU DON'T HAVE TO BE ZOMBIFIED TO WORK HERE, BUT IT HELPS

"Why you no sleep?" said one of the zombies.

One by one, all the zombies who'd been relaxing in comfy chairs, slowly stood up.

"You should be sleep," said another zombie.

The zombies began shuffling towards Ian.

"Sleep. Sleep. Sleep."

Ian slammed the door shut and ran away as fast as he could down the corridor. As he turned a corner, he heard the door of the zombie staffroom click open. He stopped and looked back and saw zombies spilling out into the corridor.

"Sleep. Sleep. Sleep," they all moaned, as they spotted Ian and began shuffling after him.

Ian turned and ran. This was far worse than anything Ian's extraordinary imagination had conjured up before, and this was really happening. He didn't care where he was going, he just wanted to get away. He ran deeper and deeper into Leviathan Hall until he had lost all sense of direction. Eventually, when he was sure he'd got away from the zombies, Ian slowed down and stopped. He slumped against a wall, trying to catch his breath, and that was when he saw it.

A door with a big red cross on the side and the word INFIRMARY written on it in big white letters. Ian walked over, slowly opened the door and went inside. He was relieved to discover that it was zombie-free.

The room had a horrible smell to it, like a mixture of his grandad Ian's socks and the juice that gathered at the bottom of the kitchen bin. The walls were full of shelves covered with dusty jars of all shapes and sizes. One had a label that said BLIND WORM'S STING, another had LIZARD LEGS written on it, and another said DRAGON

225

SCALES. Ian felt beads of sweat trickle down the back of his neck. He did not like this one little bit.

Ian tried to push away the awful feeling of dread that was bubbling inside his tummy and moved forwards. The light of his torch flashed onto a bed. Then the pool of light found another bed, then another, and another. In total, Ian saw five beds, all with people lying in them, under covers. He crept over and flashed his torch on the faces of the patients. He saw Mr Jagger, Ms Fluther-Smack, Hattie Lavernock and Eddie Splott. Finally, he got to the last bed.

"Ms Husk?" he whispered.

He heard a moaning sound from under the covers.

"Ms Husk? Is that you?"

Ian turned and saw a bag lying on a table next to the bed. He was certain it was the bag that Ms Husk had put her mobile phone in. He crept towards it and felt inside. His fingers found the hard, plastic casing of the mobile phone almost immediately. Someone moaned and moved in the bed.

"Ms Husk?" whispered Ian.

"I'm afraid not," said a horrible, familiar voice from underneath the covers.

Mr Grimble moved with ferocious speed, throwing off his duvet and jumping out of the bed. Ian dropped his torch onto the floor in shock.

"What do we have here then?" said Mr Grimble. "I thought we were missing someone."

Before Ian properly knew what was happening,

the infirmary door burst open and the room was
filled with candlelight and moaning as the zombies
shuffled in.

"Hold him," said Mr Grimble.

Ian felt hands pawing and grabbing at him.
He saw Mr Grimble lurch towards him holding
a handkerchief. Ian struggled to shake his head
away but it was no good. Mr Grimble clamped the

handkerchief over Ian's nose and a sweet scent filled his nostrils. All Ian's strength ebbed away and he suddenly felt very, very tired.

"That's it," said Mr Grimble softly. "Time to go bye-byes."

That was the last thing that Ian remembered hearing before he fell into a deep and dreamless sleep.

THURSDAY

# WHEN IS A MARSHMALLOW-ROASTING SAFETY PLATFORM NOT A MARSHMALLOW-ROASTING SAFETY PLATFORM?

Ian groaned and coughed. He felt awful, like someone had put his brain in a cement mixer. The last thing he could remember was being in the infirmary.

"Ms Husk?" he muttered, and heard a moan next to him.

He slowly opened his eyes and looked around. His sight was a bit blurry but he could feel that he was sitting on a hard floor and he was cold, very

231

cold. He blinked and slowly things began to swim into focus. He saw familiar wooden bars and realized, with horror, that he was sitting in the open air on the marshmallow-roasting safety platform. There was another groan beside him. Ian turned and saw that he was sitting next to Haroun and Ms Husk, and surrounding them were all the other Dreary Inkling students and teachers, all with their hands chained behind their backs.

"Welcome to the Leviathan Family Recreational Picnic and Sacrifice Area," said a voice from somewhere above Ian.

He looked up and saw Gertrude Leviathan hovering in a white dress, illuminated by the light of a round, full moon. She floated down onto the marshmallow-roasting safety platform like she

was a ghost. Around her neck, Ian could see the

amulet, which was glowing green.

"Mr Grimble, will you hurry up," she shouted. "I want to get to the good stuff."

Ian felt someone grab his arms behind him and click something cold and metallic around his wrists.

"That's them all chained to the platform, m'lady," said Mr Grimble, appearing from behind Ian.

"What on earth is going on?" groaned Ms Husk, who was beginning to come round.

"Well, we've got a full moon, some evil magic and a classful of victims," laughed Gertrude Leviathan. "Seems to me like it's cursing time."

"W-what?" said Ms Husk, woozily.

"We're trapped," whispered Ian. "You were drugged by Mr Grimble. We all were."

234

"Drugged?" said Ms Husk. "I-I don't understand, Liam?"

"Er, it's Ian," said Ian.

"Well, what's going on, Ian?" she said. "Where are we?"

"So, quite a lot has happened in the last day but essentially we're in a kind of cage, in an ancient sacrificial area, in the grounds of a house owned by an evil witch," said Ian.

"W-what?" said Ms Husk.

But before Ian could say anything else, a loud chanting interrupted him. Ian turned his head and saw a line of moaning zombies shuffle out of the woods. He felt his shoulder twitch. The zombies were no longer wearing hoods and the full hideousness of their faces was on display for all

to see. Understandably, this was quite an unsettling sight for Ian's classmates. Lots of them began to struggle, kicking their legs in a desperate attempt to escape their chains. Most started whimpering and Mr Jagger began shrieking and screaming. Amongst all the noise and terror, Ian felt something on his shoulder. The fingers of the zombie hand were unclamping themselves. Then, unseen by anyone else, the hand used its fingers as legs and crawled up through the neck of Ian's hoodie and jumped down onto the floor. Ian watched as the arm walked across the marshmallow-roasting safety platform, then leaped down into the clearing, where the zombies were shuffling about and moaning.

"Hello, handie," Ian heard one of the zombies say. "Me was wondering where you'd got to."

"N-now look here," said Ms Husk, fear quivering in her voice. "As the adult in charge of these children I demand to know what is going on."

Gertrude Leviathan threw her arms into the air.

"Silence!" she said.

Ian looked nervously around at his classmates. He saw looks of confusion and fear on their faces. But then he flexed his arm behind his back and realized something. Something incredible. Something that had happened when the zombie arm freed itself. Something that gave Ian hope.

"Your puny minds could not comprehend the majesty of my plan, even if I told you," Gertrude Leviathan continued.

Ian thought back to what he'd read in her diary.

"You want to turn us into brain-sucking zombies," he said. "Then you want us to suck out everyone else's brains in the whole world so they will be zombies too."

Gertrude Leviathan narrowed her eyes.

"Well, yes, in very basic terms that's the

238

outline of my plan," she said.

"And then," continued Ian, "as the only non-zombie, you will be able to control the world."

Gertrude Leviathan snorted.

"Alright, so you know exactly what my plan is," she said. "You are going to help me rule the world."

Mr Grimble took something out of his pocket, bowed his head and handed Gertrude Leviathan a small silver flask.

"Here is the evil smoothie," he said. "Made from the nine thorns, the devil's claw, the bat's blood, the cat's whisker and the witch's beard dandruff that the children collected on the scavenger hunt."

Some of Ian's classmates gasped.

"It has been mixed according to the recipe in

the Great Curse," continued Mr Grimble.

Gertrude Leviathan took the silver flask from him and held it up.

"Sweet, sweet evil smoothie," she said.

The silver flask glinted in the moonlight.

"After I drink this," she said, her eyes blazing, "I will be able to release the full power of the amulet and command an army of the undead."

Gertrude Leviathan popped the cork out of the flask and drank down the contents. And as she did, her amulet began to glow brighter.

"Now," she said, wiping her mouth on her sleeve. "Let me explain how this is going to work."

She turned and looked at the children.

"One by one, I'm going to place this magic amulet on each of your foreheads. It will take the life force from your bodies, turning you into zombies."

Eddie and Lenny started to cry at this terrifying news.

"Oh, don't worry," said Gertrude Leviathan, floating around the marshmallow-roasting safety platform. "The process is quite painless."

Ms Husk turned to Ian.

"What are we going to do?" she whispered, in a sad sort of voice. "Will nobody save us?"

241

Ian looked at the zombies surrounding the platform and started to imagine what it would be like to be like them. He imagined being neither dead nor living, a hollow-eyed creature that moaned and shuffled about all day. It sounded very much like Ian's fourteen-year-old cousin, who was also called Ian.

"Don't worry," he whispered. "I've got an idea."

# A HORRENDOUS PUDDLE OF AWFULNESS

Gertrude Leviathan floated above the Dreary Inkling Year 6 class. Her dirty grey hair fluttered in the wind like she was in some kind of demonic shampoo advert. Some of Ian's classmates were still weeping and whimpering at the thought of being turned into zombies. And the more they bawled, the more Gertrude Leviathan cackled. She could barely contain her joy at the thought of sacrificing a whole class of children and their teachers. Ian, though, wasn't crying or wailing. He was waiting for just the right moment to put his plan into effect.

"Goody, goody, goody," said Gertrude Leviathan, a smile seeping across her face like pus soaking into a bandage. "Grimble? I am ready. Get in position. It is time for me to take over the world."

"Pah!" Ian snorted.

Gertrude Leviathan scowled at him.

"What?" she said.

Ian turned his face away from her.

"Oh, nothing," he said. "Carry on with the Great Curse."

Gertrude Leviathan floated down and hovered right next to Ian.

"No, really, boy. What is it?" she said, clearly niggled by him. "You snorted. There was snorting. Why did you snort?"

"Oh, I was just thinking that you won't," said Ian, trying to stop his whole body from shaking so that she wouldn't see how scared he was.

Gertrude Leviathan lowered herself so that her face was right next to Ian's.

"Won't?" she said. "Won't what?"

"You won't rule the world," he said. "I was just thinking to myself that you won't rule the world."

Gertrude Leviathan frowned.

"What did you say?"

"I said you're not going to take over the world,"

said Ian again. "Because you're too stupid. You're a terrible witch."

"I am not a terrible witch," said Gertrude Leviathan.

Ian thought he saw a flicker of doubt cross her awful, radioactive eyes.

"Yes, you are," he said. "You tried this once before and ended up with an army of vegetarian zombies."

He took a deep breath and braced himself for what he was about to say.

"You were rubbish at spells on your sixteenth birthday and you're rubbish now."

Gertrude Leviathan stared at Ian as though her eyes were going to pop out of her head.

"SILENCE!" she screamed and pointed a finger

at one of the zombies. Her amulet suddenly glowed so brightly that Ian had to squint. "I AM NOT RUBBISH AT SPELLS!"

Gertrude Leviathan mumbled something and lightning flashed out of her fingers, hitting the zombie right between the eyes. The zombie moaned and Ian's classmates screamed. In an instant, the zombie turned into a toad that hopped away into the trees. Ian looked at Gertrude Leviathan, his teeth chattering with fear.

"Whatever," he said with a shrug, pretending that he didn't care.

"Why, you horrid little brat," said Gertrude Leviathan, who looked a little rattled at Ian's goading. "Just for that, I'm going to make you the first soldier in my zombie army."

247

She took the glowing jade amulet from around her neck and started chanting incantations into the cold night. The zombies who were standing around the outside of the marshmallow-roasting safety platform began to chant and stamp their feet. Mr Grimble walked around behind Ian and grabbed his head, holding it tight.

"The time has come," said Gertrude Leviathan, placing the stone against Ian's forehead. "A new army of the undead will be born."

Ian struggled but Mr Grimble's grip was too strong. The zombie chanting and stamping got louder and louder. Ian could feel a prickly heat begin to radiate from his head all the way through his body. Suddenly, green beams of light shot out of the amulet.

"Ian?"

He heard Ms Husk call his name, or maybe it was someone else, he wasn't very sure. The marshmallow-roasting safety platform began to melt into the background and Ian felt all woozy and tired. Images flashed through his mind. The time when he first saw Luna Axminster and his tummy went all squirty. The world record attempt to try and eat ten bananas in three

249

minutes that resulted in an unexpected and rather violent redecorating of the downstairs hall. His fourth birthday party when he'd peed in a clown's shoes. Images from his life just kept flashing in front of his eyes. It was like the amulet was sucking his memories out of his head, taking all the things from him that made him Ian Iansson.

Suddenly, Ian remembered where he was and what was happening. He looked up at Gertrude Leviathan, her face contorted and twisted in evil enjoyment and he knew that this was his chance.

"Your mother was right," he shouted, summoning every scrap of strength left in his body. "She said you'd never make it as a witch."

Gertrude Leviathan looked at him, and a look of confusion and anger flashed across her face.

Mr Grimble's grip on Ian's head slackened and at that exact moment, Ian did something that no one was expecting. He freed his hands from the chains and pulled them from behind his back. When Mr Grimble had fastened the chains around his wrists, he'd wrapped them around the zombie arm too. Once it had gone, there was enough slack in the chains for Ian to free himself. Ian grabbed hold of the amulet and in one swift movement, pulled it off his head and attached it to Mr Grimble's.

"What's going on?" screamed Mr Grimble, as the amulet glowed more intensely than ever.

Ian yanked on the amulet's chain that Gertrude Leviathan was still holding, so that she toppled forwards into Mr Grimble. The two of them fell on

251

the floor holding each other. Ian rolled for cover as great green streaks of light shot out of them. The intense heat was too much for Mr Grimble's waxy body. He screamed as his skin and bones began turning back into earwax. His face melted away and his eyeballs fell out of his skull and plopped on the floor. Eventually, all that remained of him was a pile of clothes and a large waxy puddle. Gertrude Leviathan's body shook as the magic took its course.

"Look!" said Drishya Samode, after the amulet stopped glowing.

Gertrude Leviathan moaned. She was completely covered in Mr Grimble. Slowly, she sat up, the amulet falling from her forehead. Her skin had become a strange greeny-grey colour and a spider crawled out from her right nostril, scuttled across her cheek and into her left earhole.

"My body all hurty," she said. "Me want to eat brains."

She tried to rub her head but ended up knocking it off her shoulders. It hung like a disgusting hood from the back of her neck, held onto her body by sinew and veins.

One of the zombies shuffled up the steps and put her head back on her neck.

"Hello," he said. "Don't worry about head. It fall off all the time."

A vacant smile spread across Gertrude Leviathan's face and one of her eyeballs fell out.

Everyone started cheering and chanting Ian's name.

"IAN. IAN. IAN."

Ian felt a surge of happiness jolt through his body. He turned and smiled at Ms Husk.

"I don't feel at all well," she said, and was suddenly and quite violently sick, adding to the horrendous puddle of awfulness on the marshmallow-roasting safety platform's floor.

254

# GOODBYES

The Leviathan Hall dining room was full of excited chatter. Ian was sitting with Beano and Haroun and filling them in on exactly what he'd discovered in the library and how he knew Gertrude Leviathan was a witch. The rest of Ian's classmates had gathered around and were listening to the story and laughing in all the right places.

"What happened next, Ian?"

"Were you really scared, Ian?

"What's your favourite shape, Ian?"

Everyone knew exactly who he was and what his name was and it felt amazing. It was Ms Husk who first noticed something was a bit odd.

"Ian?" she said. Even she had started to remember his name. "You look ever so peaky. Are you feeling alright?"

She pulled out a small mirror from her bag and passed it to him.

Ian looked at himself in the mirror. His face was a strange greeny-grey colour.

"I think I'm part-zombie," he said. "It must be from when the amulet was on my head."

"Oh, my goodness," said Ms Husk. "I shall get you to a hospital immediately."

Ian smiled.

"No way," he said. "It's completely awesome."

He pulled his left hand off his wrist and put it on the table. Everyone watched as the hand stood up, using its fingers as legs, grabbed a chickpea fritter from a plate, and scuttled back to Ian.

"Cool," said Beano, as Ian picked up his hand, twisted it back on his wrist and began munching away on the fritter.

"That is such a good look," said Luna Axminster,

smiling at Ian in a way that made him choke on the fritter.

"Right," shouted Ms Husk. "The coach is in the car park. I want everyone on it now, please."

Most of Dreary Inkling Year Six followed Ms Husk out of the dining room. Ian remained seated.

"You okay?" said Haroun, scraping his chair under the table.

"Sure," said Ian. "There's something I've got to do. Save me a seat on the coach, okay?"

Haroun nodded and ran out of the dining room, leaving Ian all alone.

"You sure you're okay?" said Remington Furious III, appearing in a puff of smoke.

Ian nodded.

"I can't believe I'm a zombie," said Ian.

"Part-zombie," corrected Remington Furious III. "You know, I'm sure there must be a spell in the library to turn you back into just a boy."

"Nah," he said. "I like it. People notice me. Besides, I'd always imagined that something like this would happen to me. It's great."

Ian started walking out of the dining hall.

"You were amazing," said Remington Furious III. "The way you saved everyone. It was totally incredible."

Ian smiled as he walked out of Leviathan Hall. He watched as his classmates ran out to the coach and scrambled on board. He chuckled at the sight of the driver attempting, without success, to tell everyone the rules that she expected them to follow.

259

Remington Furious III hoisted a rucksack onto his shoulder.

"Well, Ian," he said. "I think I should be leaving you now."

Ian nodded.

"Where will you go?"

Remington Furious III put on a pair of oversized sunglasses. They complemented his floral beach shirt with rainbow sleeves and multi-coloured dungarees perfectly.

"I don't know," he said. "Wherever the wind takes me, I guess. That's how I found you."

Ian wanted to tell Remington Furious III that he loved him, that he would always remember him, even when he was really old, like thirty-three or something. He wanted to tell him how

260

much he had meant to Ian, that he'd been there when he needed him the most, before he found some friends, before he had become a part-zombie. But he didn't have to, because Remington Furious III was part of Ian and so he knew all of that.

"You've got a helluva imagination, Ian," he said. "Don't let go of it, not ever. Hold on as tight as you can and use it every chance you get. People get boring because they forget how to imagine. Don't let that happen to you."

Ian nodded.

"I won't, I promise," he said, tapping his head. "My brain is completely fine and non-zombified."

He turned and saw Haroun and Beano get on the coach.

"It's just that I think I want to hang out with real people now," he said.

Remington Furious III smiled.

"I know," he said. "And I understand."

Remington Furious III held his fist to his head in salute.

"Goodbye, my friend," he said, slowly starting to drift upwards.

"Goodbye, Remington Furious III," said Ian softly, as he watched his imaginary friend float up and away into the sky. "You're the best."

Ian stood for a moment then walked down the large stone steps towards the coach where Ms Husk was waiting for him. He was quite surprised to see Gertrude Leviathan there too. She had a collar around her neck and was being held on a lead by one of the zombies.

"She wants to say goodbye," said Ms Husk.

"Me want to eat your brains," said Gertrude Leviathan.

Ian reached into his pocket and pulled out a

packet of anti-bacterial handwipes that his mum had made him bring.

"Here," he said. "These are much tastier."

Gertrude Leviathan sniffed them.

"Lemon-scented," she said. "Me like lemons. And brains."

Ms Husk nodded towards the zombie who was holding her.

"Keith here has been telling me that he's got big plans for Gertrude Leviathan and Leviathan Hall."

Keith looked at Ian.

"Me taking her to live in cage in indoor pool room," he said. "She going to keep Daisy company. Daisy will probably eat her. She like that. Then me and other zombies turn Leviathan Hall into

264

vegetarian restaurant. We will also do some vegan dishes."

Ms Husk smiled.

"I think Keith has got everything under control."

With that, Keith led Gertrude Leviathan off to live with Daisy.

Ms Husk's phone beeped.

"Oh, Ian," she said. "It's from your mum. I hope it's not too disappointing for you."

She handed Ian her phone. It said SAD NEWS FOR IAN IANSSON. DAD DID NOT GET JOB. KEPT SAYING, "UNEXPECTED ITEM IN THE

265

GAGGING AREA." WE WILL BE STAYING IN DREARY INKLING. PLEASE BREAK IT TO HIM GENTLY.

"I'm sorry," said Ms Husk.

Ian smiled and walked up the stairs onto the coach. Excitement was already bubbling at the thought of the journey back to Dreary Inkling.

"Ian, Ian, come and sit here," yelled Elton Gweek.

"Ian, sit over here," shouted Lenny Frisby.

"Ian, sit next to me," called Betty Gabalfa.

Ian smiled and high-fived people as he walked all the way to the very back of the coach where Beano and Haroun had saved him a seat by the window. Everyone was laughing and singing songs. As the coach left Leviathan Hall, Ian looked out of the window, back towards the grounds. He smiled at the thought of what incredible adventures were yet to come with all his new friends, as he watched a gigantic man with green hair float up into the bright blue sky.

"For fans of awesomeness."
DERMOT O'LEARY

"Brilliantly bonkers... hits all the right comedy buttons."
LANCASHIRE EVENING POST

"I didn't want to stop reading."
FRANCESCO, AGED 9

"The kind of book that makes everything feel not just all right but better."
PIERS TORDAY

"This book was a great success!"
GEORGE, AGED 9

CHECK OUT MORE LAUGH-OUT-LOUD

BONKERS ADVENTURES FROM...

# Dreary Inkling
# ★ SCHOOL ★

JULY 2019

BY
# Matt Brown
ILLUSTRATED BY PACO SORDO

# INCREDIBLE FACTS ABOUT DREARY INKLING PRIMARY SCHOOL

**1.** Dreary Inkling was originally known as Reary Stinkling. This is because it was founded by Vikings who used it as a toilet.

**2.** There is a wheelie-bin at the back of Dreary Inkling Primary School that no one has ever been able to open. Legend has it that the pupil who can lift the lid will become King or Queen of the school.

**3.** Dreary Inkling Primary School was opened in 1991 by the then Mayor, Mr Rollo Koster. In 1997, the new science lab was opened by Mayor Tara Dactill. And in 2002, the new school canteen was opened by Mayor Chris P. Bacon.

**4.** The school librarian is called Mrs Pinhead. No one has ever seen her, but you can detect where she is due to a powerful aroma of shortbread and danger.

**5.** There are one thousand eight hundred and seventy-eight holes in the school playground. According to a rumour started by Terence Freckleton from Year Two, one of the holes goes directly to the centre of the earth.

# FANKS

## (ACKNOWLEDGEMENTS)

Hello. This is Keith the zombie. Matt Brown want to say some fank yous and has asked me to type them up for him. I love typin' fings on the computer. Look at this.

W;EDJB;WEKJBNQWL;EDJB;WEFJHW;EJKFH;EWKJHQW;K
EFJH;WEJKFH;DJ;WEJFH;WEJLFH;WEFHJ;WEFHJQ..

Ha ha ha.

Okay. First, Matt Brown want to say a grate big FANKS to non-zombie Darcy Marie-Butler who came up wiv the AMAZING name Beano Lerwick. Wel dun, Darcy.

Next, Matt Brown want to fank all the non-zombies at Usborne who ar grate and only took out one or two jokes that were too rude or litigious, whatever that mean. So, fank you to Becky, Sarah S, Steph, Gareth, Will, Sarah C, Kat, Mariesa and Liz.

Matt Brown also want to say FANKS to family non-zombies Liz, Joe and Sam. He say that they are the best and wivout them he would just sit in his boring pants all day watching daytime TV.

Finally, Matt Brown want to fank his agent non-zombie Jenny Savill, who is also grate and makes him feel good about himself when she probably just want to have a bowl of beetroot soup and sum peace and quiet.

M;PQWERFJBEW;JKFDNBQW;OEFJN2EO;'FNW;EJNES;F,M
NQBWE;ROJBV;W3OEJFBN;WQJKENF';2WEJFNA;WOFHEOWI
FHEFIJWhw;EKJHF;ESKJNF';L/KWN'EFK.

HA HA HA HA HA.